SOUVENIRS

SOUVENIRS

W. D. WETHERELL

RANDOM HOUSE NEW YORK

Grateful acknowledgment is made to the following for
permission to reprint previously published material:

Holt, Rinehart and Winston: Four lines from "Canis Major" from
The Poetry of Robert Frost edited by Edward Connery Lathem.
Copyright 1928, © 1969 by Holt, Rinehart and Winston.
Copyright © 1956 by Robert Frost. Reprinted by permission of
Holt, Rinehart and Winston, Publishers.

Portions of this novel appeared in a different form, entitled
"Past Things," in the Fall 1978 issue of *Carolina Quarterly.*

Library of Congress Cataloging in Publication Data

Wetherell, W. D., 1948–
Souvenirs.

I. Title.
PS3573.E9248S6   813'.54   81–1103
ISBN 0–394–51662–1   AACR2

Manufactured in the United States of America

24689753

FIRST EDITION

For my mother and my father

"Peoples without a past need souvenirs . . ."
—HENRI DE MOTHERLANT

SOUVENIRS

**I** She was not a woman given to secret ambitions, but if one had been demanded of her, say at a party, one of the impromptu college parties she had gone to before her mother set fire to the house, it would have been to have an advertisement in the Sunday magazine section of *The New York Times.* Toward the back preferably, somewhere between the crossword puzzle and the letters column. She could see it as vividly as if it were a slide projected on the wall behind the folding chairs she had provided for her two visitors to sit on: at the top, there would be a montage of rusty jackknives, tattered post cards and other accumulated treasures that might be found in a forgotten drawer; at the bottom, a coupon that could be clipped and sent to her; in between, large blocks of the old-fashioned type that had advertised sarsaparilla a century before.

THE PAST PATCHED UP! it would read. *Scrapbooks Our Specialty. Old Uniforms Darned, Bootees Bronzed, Love Letters Framed and Mounted. Home Movies Preserved. An Elaine Splice Is a Good Splice! Negatives Cleaned, Baby Books Edited. Spruce Up a Memory for Christmas.*

But she hadn't got very far with the ad—a telephone call to find out how much it would cost, a few random sketches on the legal pad she kept on her desk in an attempt to seem organized. She reached for the pad now, trying to concentrate on what Mr. Powers was telling her, trying to block out the steady tapping sound on the ceiling as her mother, in the midst of one of her imaginary shopping expeditions through the apartment upstairs, came to the spot where the living-room carpet ended and the kitchen linoleum began. It was one-thirty now. Her mother's lunch was a half-hour overdue.

Mr. Powers raised his eyes toward the ceiling and smiled. "My mother."

"Of course," Mr. Powers murmured. "Of course." And he smiled again.

Mr. and Mrs. Powers were exactly the sort of well-dressed, affluent couple that she had originally imagined would comprise her clientele. That was years ago, back in the days when there was a freshly painted sign outside the house that read "Collier Antiques" and she still had illusions about moving into Manhattan from Queens. She had felt a moment of recognition when the Powers first came in, the nostalgic kind of anger someone feels when faced with a dream arriving a decade too late. Even now, though they had brought no Chippendale chair or Victorian snuff box or said a word about antiques, there was something in the concerned, overly careful way Mr. Powers treated his wife that made Elaine think of a man tenderly carrying a priceless vase for her to repair, afraid that any second it might shatter.

Like most of her clients, they had found her through word-of-mouth, in this case through Helen Tousignant, a friend of Elaine's from college whose antique business in Connecticut attracted the estate-in-Greenwich, boiler-factory-in-Bridgeport type of person. Now that Elaine's original hopes were gone, she found she had little patience with people who dressed and talked the way they did. Her father had been killed in Korea when she was six, and things had never been easy for her. But at least, since Helen had already told them, she wouldn't have to explain what it was she was offering them.

"I patch up the past," she used to say to the men just out of college who stammered some compliment about her silky black hair and invariably found it necessary to ask her permission before reaching across the table to take her hand.

"Oh, you're an archaeologist!" they would say, launching into what little they remembered about ancient Greece. And it was true she had taken a course in that department, taught by a handsome man in his early fifties who called her Nefertiti in class and stared at her in a way that left her feeling excited and confused.

"I patch up the past," she explained later to the middle-aged businessmen in the city she met through friends who typed in their offices, men who said nice things about her high cheekbones and complained about her lack of make-up in the same breath.

"You're an antique restorer," they would say over dinner, their legs pressing hers under the table. This was close to the mark. She had intended to specialize in that field, and it was less a deliberate decision than the multiple promptings and pressures of fate that had caused the alteration in her design.

"I patch up the past," she would explain to the few men she stumbled into after that, men who made sarcastic jokes about the tortoise-shell glasses she wore instead of contact lenses, or the spinsterish bun in which she caught her hair, cynical men who would ask her back to their apartments and sulk like little boys when she told them no.

"You're a mortician," they said. "You pretty up the dead for the rest of us, and you've been doing it for so long you've forgotten what it means to be alive."

She always had to explain. People never got it right, especially at first. Their misunderstanding was in some respects the basis of her career. Interested in art but with no talent for drawing, fascinated by history but with no inclination to teach, a collector without the means to collect, she had decided to go into antique restoration before the end of her sophomore year, choosing her courses thereafter with an eye toward their utility in getting her started. In the same purposeful, optimistic way, she had converted the first floor of her mother's house in Woodhaven into a workshop and office, convincing herself that the quiet rows of two-family homes that spread for blocks on either side would provide an untapped reservoir of antiques in need of repairs. Antiques in need of her.

And she actually had worked on a few. There was a Victorian marble-topped chest with a crack down one side from being used as a stickball backstop by the owner's son; a nineteenth-century Amish quilt a widow had been using to wrap her dachshund in so he wouldn't get cold; some Colonial candlestick holders that were badly tarnished, brought in by an old friend of the family who felt sorry for her and wanted to help. She had been polishing these, trying to stretch the work out to fill a day, when destiny arrived in the unlikely guise of Mr. and Mrs. Adolph Shugrue, standing at the door with their burlap bag like elderly trick-or-treaters come to beg.

"Are you the antique-fixing lady?" they asked.

She had sat them down in the same chairs the Powers were using now. Without saying anything, Mr. Shugrue had dumped the bag's contents across her otherwise empty desk.

"Our heirloom crockery," Mrs. Shugrue announced over the rattle, managing to sound proud and heartbroken at the same time. "It's busted."

There were shards of various colors, shapes and sizes: marble-brown, bluish-gray; jagged triangles, little squares. Whether because of the dust or the fuzzy patina of brown over the cracks, Elaine had never seen anything that so immediately conveyed a sense of great age.

"How old are these?" she asked carefully, trying to hide her excitement.

Mrs. Shugrue looked at Mr. Shugrue. Mr. Shugrue shrugged.

"I don't know," he said. "Thirty years. Thirty-five. You too young to remember John Garfield? Betty Grable? That's when."

"We got them at the movies," Mrs. Shugrue explained. "You went to the matinee, you got a saucer. Come back at night, you got the cup. This one used to belong to our girl Betty. The crack is where she broke it the time she flunked math. We want it all fixed up nice again."

Elaine tried to explain that damaged dinnerware from the

1940's wasn't exactly her line, but they refused to understand. Each sliver and chip held a different memory, and they made her listen while they went through quarrels of a generation ago, dwelling on clumsy accidents that had seemed tragic at the time, laughing over crazy parties where people now dead had once raised hell. She had no choice after that. Rather than hurt their feelings, she told them to leave the china with her and come back in two weeks. As soon as they were gone, she swept the pieces into a shoe box, feeling guilty at her weakness but taking comfort from the thought that the cups and saucers were, if nothing else, an unsurpassed example of true Americana.

What was strange was that the longer she kept the Shugrue's treasure, the more appealing it seemed, especially in comparison to the genuine antiques resting next to it on the shelf. The vases and candlestick holders were much older, of course, but they were shiny and cold, with no trace of the past; they warded off time's stain as if they were protected by a special shellac. The crockery, on the other hand, seemed to absorb memories, making the coffee-stained fragments richer and more suggestive than the sterile brass or porcelain. Elaine had respect for the antiques and took pride in restoring them, but piecing the crockery back together, she felt that she was re-creating the past itself.

The Shugrues were delighted with the results. They brought her some cracked ashtrays from the 1939 World's Fair; they recommended her to friends. It didn't take long for word to spread. Where before she had sat alone for hours on end with nothing to do, she suddenly had so many clients she had to turn some away. Almost accidentally, half against her will, she had stumbled upon a great need.

"I patch up the past," she said out of habit, swiveling back to face the Powers. "I patch up the past, and quite frankly my fees are very high."

Mr. Powers was turning through the pages of an old scrapbook Elaine had left on the work bench. He shrugged, as if to say "of course" again. It was remarkable, now that she thought of it, how much he had managed to convey to her through gesture and expression alone in the half-hour or so he and his wife had been there. From time to time there was his nod toward Mrs. Powers, who sat on the verge of tears in the chair nearest the desk ("Humor her"); there was his shake of the head ("I know what you think of us, but we need your help"), the finger pressed gently to his lips to stop something she was about to say, quickly followed by the smile to smooth away any embarrassment the silence might have caused. He and I are like lovers, she thought, sharing our own secret language that no one else can ever know.

"We'd just like to have his belongings neatened a bit," Mrs. Powers said in a broken voice. "There really is so much. John was a very photogenic boy."

John was their son, their only child. He had been shot through the forehead leading a patrol near the Demilitarized Zone in Vietnam in 1968. Elaine hadn't been able to hide her surprise when they told her. Whatever else they were, they were not the kind of people who permitted their son to be drafted.

"It's been thirteen years now," Mrs. Powers whispered. "Thirteen years next Thursday, and there hasn't been a single moment in all that time when I've been able to keep myself from thinking about him. I've tried Valium. I've even tried . . ."

She didn't finish. She let her head drop toward her shoulder, reminding Elaine of a mechanical doll whose spring has suddenly worn out. There was something doll-like about her appearance, too. Her vivid green eyes could have been glass. Her complexion had the perfection of china, needing some vital spark to bring it to life. Even her grief seemed artificial. She sat there twisting her handkerchief as if trying to remember the proper gestures for bereavement as demonstrated in an old issue of *Vogue*.

"We've brought a few things to show you," Mr. Powers said. "Just a sampling of what there is at home."

The "things" were in a wicker picnic basket: a few scrapbooks, a baby book with the inevitable envelope of silky curls; a toy or two; a formal photograph taken at John's graduation from prep school in New Hampshire. He was handsome in the same unlikely way his father was: wavy blond hair, inward-staring eyes, a squarish face, a nose a bit too large for the squareness to carry off. While Elaine went through the basket, Mr. Powers sat holding his wife's hand, rubbing one finger along his forehead as if he were aware of the resemblance and secretly ashamed of it.

"There are boxes more at home," he said. "Mrs. Powers can't bear parting with them for more than a day or two at most. Naturally, that must be taken into account."

"Naturally," said Elaine.

She reached into the basket and took out a toy airplane. The paint was peeling. The propeller had rusted and wouldn't spin. Mrs. Powers explained it had once been John's favorite toy. He'd had pneumonia the winter he was five and had to stay in bed. All day he spun the propeller, pretending to make the plane fly, refusing to let them exchange it for any other toy.

"It used to be such a pretty blue color," Mrs. Powers said. "Blue like the sky."

"It made a humming noise when you turned the prop," Mr. Powers added. "I think that's what he liked about it."

Elaine pushed it experimentally across her desk. One of the wheels fell off.

"New wheel. New paint. New propeller," Elaine said, writing on her pad. "That shouldn't be hard."

The two clocks on the bookcase struck the hour, each in turn, the first notes of the second blending into the last notes of the first. Upstairs, her mother had stopped pacing. The silence worried Elaine. At least with the footsteps she could keep track of where she was.

Mr. Powers said something to his wife about her being more comfortable outside while they discussed the arrangements in detail. Elaine suggested a coffee shop across the street.

"Carol?"

"Yes, dear?"

"Why don't you leave the airplane here with us?"

Mrs. Powers reached into her pocketbook like someone accidentally caught shoplifting.

"How silly of me. You will take care of it, won't you, Miss Collier? You'll remember what I said about the blue?"

"Sky blue. I'll remember."

"Well, good-by then. Across the street you said?"

Mr. Powers helped her to the door. When he came back, he was shaking his head.

"As you can see, she's heartbroken over losing him," he said. "There was no reason for him to die, but that's beside the point. He's dead and has been dead for some time. The important one now is Carol. She has responsibilities and obligations to meet. We maintain a large house. In my position one must do a certain amount of entertaining. Life goes on. In short, her suffering has to come to an end before—and I'm not exaggerating here, Miss Collier—before it kills her as well."

"Aren't you being a bit melodramatic?" Elaine asked. "It's not the first time a mother has lost a son."

"Granted. But it's *my* wife and *my* son we're talking about. My wife looks through these scrapbooks constantly. The home movies we have of John are her entire life."

"All right, I can patch them up for you. That's what you want, isn't it?"

Mr. Powers moved his head slightly in a gesture that could have been either a shrug or a nod. For the first time Elaine noticed that he was suffering, too, even more intensely than his wife. He looked at the picnic basket, then quickly turned to face the window, slapping at his pant legs as if to brush away the few dusty sunbeams gathered near his cuffs. Ever since she was a little girl, Elaine had always imagined what everyone she met would look like if they were in tears. Mr. Powers, she had decided when she first saw him, wasn't capable of crying at all. Now, she wasn't so sure. There was a tenseness about him that, given the right stimulus, might find relief in sobs, the desperate, gulping kind that would shake his entire body. She wondered if he had cried when the message came about John.

"Carol tried a seance once," he said. "Without telling me, of course. Above a little shop in Greenwich Village. It's a miracle she wasn't mugged."

"Did he appear?"

This time the sarcasm worked. She saw him wince. His hand tightened around his shoe.

"As a matter of fact, he didn't. The lady who ran it said the atmosphere wasn't right. She told Carol to come back the following day with a certified check. But you must understand, the problem isn't making him appear, it's making him disappear."

"Disappear?" Elaine was startled.

"If only we could find some way of making her forget John, making her forget so gradually that it would seem, in the end, as though she had never really lost him at all."

"I'm afraid you've come to the wrong person, Mr. Powers. I'm in the business of helping people remember, not forget."

"That's too bad," he said. "The way the world is nowadays, you'd do a lot better the other way around."

"Helping people forget?"

"It's the easiest thing in the world."

She didn't know whether or not he meant it as a joke. She usually felt very much in command during her interviews with clients, but from the very start Mr. Powers had given her the feeling that he was setting the tone, leading her in directions she wasn't sure she wanted to go.

"Sometimes I think it's John's belongings she remembers, not John himself," he said softly.

"I still don't understand, Mr. Powers. What exactly is it you want me to do with these?"

"Why, patch them up, of course, What else could I mean?"

"You said something about making him disappear?"

"We won't worry about that right now," he said. "I think the important thing is for her to learn to trust you."

"You'll be bringing more of his things then?"

"We have them stored away in trunks. I'll bring them down myself. It's an hour's drive from Greenwich."

"Very well," Elaine said. "I'll work on these as soon as I have time. It's a busy period for me right now."

"No hurry. In fact, the longer you take on them, the better."

Again Elaine wasn't sure what he meant.

Mr. Powers stood up to leave. "Helen neglected to mention that you were so young and attractive. Oh, I'm sorry, does that embarrass you? It's just that we both pictured a little old craftsman of some sort. A gray-haired cobbler."

"Hardly," she said.

They both laughed, even though it wasn't particularly funny. It seemed to make it easier for him. As he buttoned his overcoat, he told her how his son had come to be killed.

"Just a routine patrol, you understand. A village, some children taunting his men. He was a lieutenant. Ten months he was there. A muddy village. Whistles, shouts. And then those awful people just shot him. Shot him like a dog."

"What month in 1946 was he born?" Elaine asked suddenly.

"February. How did . . ." He reached for the graduation picture on the desk and turned it over. "It's not on the back," he said, puzzled. "Carol didn't say what year he was born, did she? How did you know?"

"I was born in 1946, too. In March. You get so you can tell after a while."

He looked at her. "Oh, I see," he said unconvincingly.

He glanced at his watch and reached across the desk to shake her hand. Since there was so much work involved, he understood that the fee would be somewhat higher than her usual one, he said, and he was prepared . . . But for some reason she told him that it would be only her usual fee.

"Fine. The coffee shop?"

"Two doors down to the right."

"Good-by, Miss Collier. I'll be in touch."

"Good-by, Mr. Powers. Mr. Powers?"

"Yes?"

"I think you better leave the airplane here with me."

At first he looked at her as if he didn't understand. He pressed his hand against his jacket pocket like someone checking to see whether his wallet was still there.

"I didn't realize I had it," he said sheepishly. He put it upside down on her work bench. "I guess old things become everything after a while."

"Good-by, Mr. Powers."

The moment he left, she went upstairs to make sure her mother was all right. The last footsteps she had heard had been on the squeaky floorboards of the hall near the bathroom. She looked in there first to make sure the medicine cabinet was still locked and her mother hadn't played with the faucets. After that she checked the kitchen. She'd had the range changed from gas to electric after the fire, but she still had to be careful. The day before she had come upstairs and found her mother cooking an empty saucepan, stirring it with her index finger in the belief that she was making pudding.

But this time, the stove was off. The windows were locked. There was no sign of anything wrong. As usual, her mother had left her a note. It was written in orange crayon on paper she had torn from a shopping bag, taped to the refrigerator door where Elaine would be sure to see it.

"Dear Elaine," it read, "I'm off to watch the parade for Lucky Lindy down Broadway. I'll be back for dinner. Your loving Mother."

Elaine peeled the tape off the door and put the note in the drawer with the others. The doctors at the clinic liked to look at them; they had said something about encouraging her in her smaller delusions. One of the notes had been about going off to see the *Hindenburg* land in Brooklyn, another had been about visiting a cousin who had died in 1936. What they meant was that her mother was taking a nap.

Elaine peeked in the bedroom door to make sure. Just as she expected, her mother was curled up on her bed with a pillow, dreaming. She seemed flushed but happy. She was making little flipping motions with her hands, like someone throwing confetti.

"Mommy?" Elaine whispered.

She was really asleep this time, not pretending—it would be safe to leave her alone for another hour or two at least. Elaine reminded herself to remember to ask how the parade had been that night at dinner, then went downstairs to her workshop, leaving the bedroom door open so she could hear if something went wrong in the dream and her mother should start to scream.

The Powers were the only appointment she had made for the day. Major Haig-Brown's service medals were awaiting a thorough polish; a retired elementary-school principal had brought over some badly peeled oil paintings, and a Mr. and Mrs. Hill had come all the way down from White Plains with the uniforms they had worn in World War II, he in the Marines, she in the Army nurse corps, the two of them having tried them on in a sentimental mood and discovered that moths had gotten at the sleeves.

It was widows and widowers mostly these days, people wanting their old films spliced together into continuous reels, rips repaired, smudges erased. Elaine sat at the new splicing machine she'd ordered from Japan, running their lives through the viewfinder, dabbing with a camel's-hair brush to remove particles of dirt from the necks of babies being bounced by grandparents who were twenty years dead, smoothing out a baby gently pushed toward a waiting father's arms, a sentimental father who had saved so hard to buy the camera in the first place and who now—a widower living on a small pension—brought her the films to be cleaned on the advice of a woman in the Council on Aging office, his children all having moved to California years before.

There were the films, and there were the love letters. People were inevitably shy when they handed over the latter, apologetic and defensive at the same time. "These are silly," they would say, pulling rubber bands off the shoe box. "We wrote these when we were kids, we've kept them all these years, please don't laugh at us." They would begin to explain how they had first met, all the circumstances involved in various silly quarrels, how their different nicknames had first evolved.

Elaine would leaf through the letters first to see what kind of paper she was dealing with—standard typing paper wore best; perfumed stationery often spoiled—then rearrange them in chronological order, taping torn ones back together, reuniting pages that had somehow got separated, brushing up the ink on signatures across the bottom. Experience had taught her that lovers, no matter how fast they scribbled the rest of the letter, always took pains with the very end, as if by delicacy and precision they could make the last words convey the sincerest affection of all. As a result, the pen would be held more lightly, less ink would be used. It inevitably became the first part of the letter to fade. Elaine would have to rummage through her desk for the proper kind of pen and forge new endings for them herself. "Love, Charlie," she would write, practicing over and over again on a piece of yellow scrap paper until she had it right. "Love, Clara;" "Kisses, Beau;" "Constantly, Todd." Over and over again, name after name, until eventually she became expert at forging the word "love" in all its variations; a specialist in the sentimental endearments of a half century ago.

The scrapbooks were more time-consuming but somehow purer. She had once repaired one for a man who was the fourth person in the United States to have a private pilot's license; another for an aging soprano who had sung Isolde at the Met. These interested her in a way the movies and love letters did not. The pictures of lean, boyish fliers standing proudly next to their kitelike planes; the autographs of great singers scrawled across dusty programs of long-forgotten matineés challenged her ability to resurrect—to freshen the gloss on old black-and-white prints until the fliers appeared in all their optimism and naïveté; to mend the rips in the libretti until their hint of baroque grandeur was as good as new. She was nothing if not thorough. Before she went to work she would read everything she could find on the early days of aviation, listen to recordings of Melchior and Flagstad singing Wagner, have all these atmospheres behind her before even touching a print or a page.

"Well, I'll be damned," the pilot had said when she returned his scrapbook to him at the nursing home. "There's Jack Peters! I'd forgotten about him. Christ, he was a crazy son-of-a-gun. There was that time he ground-looped a Jenny out at Curtiss Field."

"Yes," the soprano whispered, closing her eyes, running her pale fingers along the program as if feeling Braille. "Yes, I can see it now. The circle of seats and faces, the footlights . . . This great huge man towering over me, singing like a god."

Even the mundane scrapbooks fascinated her. Newspaper clippings that must have seemed terribly significant at the time ("Roosevelt Promises Fighting Man a New Deal"); magazine pictures of the first atomic bomb explosion pasted on a page next to graduation portraits of a pathetically small high-school class; silly love letters taped carefully next to torn ticket stubs, below and to the right of old corsages, brown now, like brittle bits of dead leaf, above and to the left of faded menus with the dishes that had been ordered checked off in lipstick. Snapshots farther back, people in white flannel posing with a cow whose head was sticking through a fence (where was the cow, she wondered; where were the people; where was the fence); girls in long dresses walking arm-in-arm toward the camera, the shy one, the one whose eyes were half-closed in all the pictures, having inevitably been the one to print the captions in India ink across the margins, the foolish captions that even Elaine couldn't read decades later without blushing for their innocence. . . . Elaine sitting there past dinner time turning pages that tore at the slightest touch, as if those memories pressed so carefully away were never actually meant to be remembered at all.

Once, not long after she had first gone into business, a middle-aged woman brought in a scrapbook she had kept on a trip across the country with her parents in 1939. Her father had been interested in seeing the Civil War battlefields; her mother, who was dying of cancer, wanted the opportunity to say good-by to her widely scattered sons.

It was a cheap leather scrapbook. The binding was torn, and Elaine had to resew it before she did anything else. Pasted on the inside cover was a picture of the three of them standing in front of an old Ford outside their farmhouse near Syracuse. "Mamma, Poppa and me, Margaret," the caption read, "started on a southern trip March 8, 1939. The first night we reached Harrisburg, Penn. and stayed overnight at Billy's. The next a.m. we started at 10 and reached Washington D.C. our nation's capital at 1:30 p.m. We looked over Washington until 5:30 then started south toward Richmond, Virg. and retired 22 miles south of Washington, D.C. at Dona's Love Nest. Next a.m. we reached Richmond then traveled directly west in Virginia to Natural Bridge. Bidding Natural Bridge farewell we went south to Bristol, Tenn. where we slept overnight. Mamma was sick here. Saturday we crossed Tenn. visiting Lookout Mountain, Chattanooga, Tenn. then into

Georgia and arriving at Irving's rooming house in Atlanta 10013 Ponce de Leon Avenue at 8:30 p.m."

Farther on there were snapshots of her standing next to a cannon atop Lookout Mountain with her arm around her mother, Margaret with a big smile, trying to convince whomever the pictures were intended for that everything was fine; her mother with a bashful little grin, her eyes on the ground as if the camera was new to her and she was afraid it might hurt. In tidying up the pictures, Elaine soon came to realize that Margaret had taken only one dress with her on the trip. She wore it in every city, with the same saddle shoes, the same baggy socks. She was pretty in the way of girls who are pretty without anyone's particularly noticing it; shy except when she was around children . . . bangs over her forehead, a little round cap on top, following fashions and trends that were probably already out of date in 1939.

It was odd the things she had thought to include. Toll receipts from the Mississippi bridges, photos of chain gangs working along the back roads, grease-stained menus from cheap diners. Pressed between two pages was a cotton plant, or at least the remnants of what had once been a cotton plant. When Elaine reached down to touch it, the dust puffed into her eyes and made her sneeze. On the next page was a picture of three small black boys standing in a road near a mule. "Little nigger boys," the caption read. "They come out to the car and jitterbug when they see white people come by. They want a quarter only Poppa said they weren't good enough for a dime!" There were pictures of the tourist cabins they had stayed in and one of her mother posing on the steps where Huey Long had been shot—smiling but vaguely nervous, as though she was afraid the gunman might still be around. In New Orleans they had gone on a steamer ride upriver. There was a picture of Margaret standing next to a lifeboat with the captain, who had put his arm around her, Margaret looking very excited and proud, the captain looking suitably handsome and complacent. Underneath the picture Margaret had written "MY BOYFRIEND" in big letters.

The photos became scarcer toward the back. Instead of being crowded six to a page, each had a page to itself. In putting the scrapbook together, Margaret had obviously started out with a tremendous burst of enthusiasm, wondering how she could possibly fit all her new experiences into one small book. Later, she had realized there wasn't enough material to fill it after all, so she had started padding it out, writing bigger captions, giving each souvenir more room. There were receipts from hospitals in various small towns, copies of prescriptions to ease her mother's pain, a cheaply printed leaflet warning about white-fringed beetles with a picture and description of what the bug looked like. Eventually, even these gave out, leaving nothing but page after empty page. Elaine was left feeling disappointed and unsatisfied, wishing there were more. For all its foolishness, the scrapbook gave her a sense of how big the country was in those years, made her feel on the verge of grasping what it was like to be a young girl raised on a farm seeing the world for the first time.

Homesick, Margaret had taken pictures along the way of cows, fields, isolated trees that, according to the caption, resembled those they had in Syracuse. They were clumsy pictures—inevitably the subject was in a corner. But bad as they were, they conveyed, in the expanse of empty land with the shade of a mountain in the distance, the stubble of young, growing wheat in the foreground, an appreciation of the tremendous promise that had once been there, a potential that nothing, not dancing black boys, old rooming houses or pathetic tourist cabins, was able to hide. Spaciousness. Fecundity. Strength. There was Margaret in bangs age nineteen; there was Margaret age fifty, alone now, knocking shyly at Elaine's door, bearing in a carefully wrapped brown package the one great adventure of her life.

There was a last photo pasted inside the back cover: Margaret in the Ford again, this time at home, sitting by herself in the front with a baby lamb in her lap, hugging it against her chest as if she would never let it go. "Wish it was my boyfriend!" the caption read, and though Elaine was not sentimental about animals and had no wish to become so emotionally involved in her work, the moment she turned to it she had burst into tears.

Three weeks went by before Elaine spoke to either of the Powers again. She hadn't worked on any of John's things during that time—there were other projects to finish first, and Mr. Powers had insisted there was no rush. He had sent another box down by parcel post, instead of delivering it in person as he had promised. This one contained John's baby things: plastic rattles and toys, birthday cards relatives had sent him for his first birthday, several studio baby pictures.

Elaine unwrapped them, feeling puzzled. They were in perfect condition; they needed no repairs whatever, not even touching up. She had just decided to call Mr. Powers to ask if there hadn't been some mistake when the phone rang.

It was Mrs. Powers, her voice high-pitched and tight, reminding Elaine of a doll again, but this time of a doll who had shattered into dozens of angry pieces.

"Where are they?" she demanded.

"Hello?" Elaine said, taken aback. "Mrs. Powers?"

"I knew we were wrong to trust you. What have you done with them?"

"You mean John's things? Why, I have them here in my workshop. I understood there was . . ."

"Those pictures and toys are all I have left of my baby, and you've stolen them, deliberately stolen them! I've just finished speaking with Mr. Powers at his office. Our lawyer will see to it that you never again have the opportunity to prey on unsuspecting people who have put their trust in you. Mr. Powers promised me you'd make repairs overnight and send them right back. It's the only reason I consented to part with them for even a minute."

"But I thought there was no hurry," Elaine said.

"No hurry! Of course there is. I must have those things back at once, understand? At once, Miss Collier! I know it must be impossible for a spinster like yourself to appreciate the feelings of a . . ."

Elaine hung up. Her first impulse was to send John's things back immediately, but for a reason she did not exactly understand she decided to go ahead with her original intention instead and call Mr. Powers at his office. There was a phone number on the check he had sent her. She had to go through a receptionist and three secretaries before she was able to talk to him.

"What a nice surprise! How are you, Miss Collier?"

"Fine. At least I was fine until your wife called."

"Carol called you? What on earth for?"

Elaine hesitated before answering. His phone voice surprised her. It had a slight lisp she hadn't noticed when they talked in person. It was the hidden sense of vulnerability beneath the smooth self-assurance that was his most attractive feature; she wondered if he knew it.

He listened to her explanation without interrupting.

"I didn't think she'd miss them so soon," he said at the end. "There are so many other things of John's she can look at. But I'm sorry she had to bother you. That part about talking to me on the phone is a complete fabrication."

"Mr. Powers, I don't want to go on working for you unless you tell me what it is I'm expected to do. I patch up old things, not marriages. I feel caught in the middle of something here, and I'd like to know what it is."

"Don't be silly. How can you stop when you haven't even started?"

"I have enough problems of my own, Mr. Powers, without getting involved in yours."

There was a pause—she heard him talking to someone in his office in the same irritated tone he had just used with her. She decided to hang up at his next angry word, but just as in their first interview, he seemed to anticipate her. When he spoke again, his voice was lower, more confidential, coaxing.

"Listen, can you hold out for another two weeks? I've got to fly to Chicago on business on Monday, but I'll be back the week after next. Why don't I plan to come to your office that Friday? You're absolutely right about my owing you an explanation."

"What about your wife?"

She didn't realize how ambiguous the question sounded until she asked it, but he seemed to interpret it the way she had meant it.

"I'll deal with Carol. I'll simply tell her you're overwhelmed with work and haven't had time for John yet. Is the Friday after next convenient with you?"

"I'm afraid you'll be wasting your time, Mr. Powers."

"Can't you wait and hear me out before deciding? I'll be there around noon."

Later that day, after she had had a chance to think some more about the Powers, it occurred to her that she might have been wrong to let the job bother her. Perhaps it wasn't that unusual after all. There was never any telling what clients wanted from their pasts. Most of them weren't satisfied with merely having their souvenirs restored. Memories changed over the years, and people wanted things changed to keep up with them. Pure restoration would have been easy, simply a matter of the proper research and the right glue. Instead it was a constant guessing game, trying to understand what people saw in old spoons from Niagara Falls, what they wanted from Union Pacific timetables preserved in a cardboard jewelry box for fifty years. She couldn't just polish the spoons, mend the paper. The burnish had to be there as well, the soft, vaguely painful, just barely endurable pull of it. It had to be there, or they demanded their money back.

Mrs. Powers' phone call had merely served to remind her that there were more and more aspects of her business that she didn't care for at all. She always felt terribly deflated, for instance, when she turned from working on other people's pasts to an examination of her own. How little there was! Two scenes really, at least where her father was concerned. There was the time she rode the subway into the city with him the day he decided—having been unsuccessful at three different jobs since his discharge from the army—to reenlist for Korea. She remembered the delightfully terrifying noise the cars made swaying back and forth on the tracks, how dark it was in the tunnel, the way he carried her piggyback up the stairs two at a time, the sudden burst of cold sunlight when they reached the top, the dwarfing skyscrapers, the boyish way her father laughed, the two of them dodging in and out of the traffic as if it were a picnic they were running to, not a war.

There was another scene, one her imagination seemed to place on the very next day. It was the time the Western Union delivery man arrived with the telegram that told them he'd been killed. Her mother was home because it was lunch hour and the office didn't need her until one, which gave her enough time to heat soup for Elaine and make sure she hadn't been playing with the gas. Elaine remembered it was split pea that day. She remembered the way the man kept looking at the tops of his shiny black shoes, the cup of cocoa she had offered him when her mother began to cry (crying, Elaine had often thought since, because the North Koreans had ended her chances for a son), the way he had said, "Well, aren't you the perfect little lady!" and picked her up to kiss her on the cheek, the quarter he'd given her. But there were no souvenirs of this occasion, no way of knowing whether she really did remember or whether the scene had been forced on her memory from hearing her mother describe it with chokes and hiccoughs so many times.

There were no relatives to take pictures of, no baby brothers or sisters, no baby books of blue or pink in which she could paste pencil outlines she'd drawn around their hands. The quarter had gone to buy a black veil she wore to church that Sunday; her father's old scrapbooks were destroyed the night her mother set fire to the house. And when her life did change—very suddenly, the year she won the scholarship and went to Boston—it changed so drastically that there seemed to be little sense in keeping a record of it. No collection of past things could reconcile the faded snapshots of an ugly, skinny, ashamed little girl sitting in front of their stoop with a broken tricycle and the precise pen-and-ink drawings students from the art department made of the twenty-year-old Elaine posing among the flowers on the banks of the Charles, her hair over her eyes, her head tilted sideways toward the blossoms.

There was no reconciling them, so she threw away all the sketches ever done of her, the patches from sorority ski trips, the theater ticket stubs. Now, when it might be nice to have something to remind her of friends her age in college, it was too late. On Tuesdays she took her mother to the clinic, and all she was reminded of was how much she had come to resemble other thirty-five-year-old women bringing their mothers in for treatment: the same shapeless woolen overcoat, heavy boots, the scarf hiding the hair none of them had time for any more, the same vague resentment and fatigue with which they picked up magazines from the waiting-room table and put them back down again unread. They were all the same in every detail save one. The others had babies in their arms; she had Major Haig-Brown's diaries which needed their bindings sewn. They held their own futures; she held other people's pasts.

There was no escaping it. Her mother lived entirely in the past now. It wasn't "Mother, please go into the hall and get a can of tuna fish from the cupboard;" it had to be, "Mommy, please walk over to Mr. Hale's on Jamaica Avenue and bring me home one of his delicious codfish." This was in her mother's docile moods. When she was upset, she would spend the entire morning in bed, muttering half-remembered slogans she'd picked up at union rallies in downtown New York during the twenties. "The Haves have the money," she would chant, pulling the bedspread over her head, "the Have Nots have the pain. We fought their war for them while moneybags played polo."

"Shh, Mommy," Elaine would say, gently tugging the blankets back down so she could see her. "That's all ancient history now."

"It's the likes of us who get kicked in the end, Elaine love," she'd whisper, not quite ready to be appeased. "Haves have the money, Have Nots have the pain."

"A mild form of latent retardation," the first doctor had said when Elaine told him about this. He was a short, raspy kind of man with Brillo-like hair who had written equations across his pad in the course of explaining to Elaine what was wrong. "A classical chemical imbalance, exacerbated by the trauma of your father's death."

"Can it be controlled?" asked Elaine.

The doctor shrugged.

"Is it hereditary?"

He shrugged again.

"What should I do with her?"

He didn't answer.

"Premature senility," the second doctor had said. "Hardening of the arteries, complicated by mental strain; i.e., your mother's unfulfilled need for a son."

This was a touchy point with Elaine. As long as she could remember, her mother had talked about what she would do when her first son was born—the names she would give him, the toys she would buy, how he would go to college when he was old enough, become a lawyer or engineer. Even as a child, Elaine had had the sense not to try to substitute for this missing "him," but had instead encouraged her mother's delusion right from the start, talking about the games she would teach "him" once he was born, promising to watch out for "him" when they played in the streets, finding, as the years went by, that it was easier to share a phantom than to compete with one.

"A severe anxiety neurosis," the third doctor explained. "You must put your mother in a home."

He had recommended one on Staten Island, calling them to make the arrangements before Elaine had time to decide whether or not it was the proper solution. "They have what's called their 'Get-Acquainted Week,'" he said, handing Elaine a mimeographed list of activities. "I've made a reservation for a single room for your mother starting next Monday."

It was a mistake, of course. Her mother cried when Elaine left. The lady in charge made Elaine sign a release giving them permission to try various tranquilizers on her, "In case she's a screamer," one of the orderlies explained when Elaine asked him about it. Her mother's room, once they got there, was little bigger than a normal bathroom. There were bars across the window and the bed was fastened to the floor with iron bolts.

It was a nightmare. Elaine forced herself to go along with the arrangements overnight, but it was too much for her—the worry, the guilt—and when the gates opened the following morning, she was waiting in the driveway to take her mother home. In talking to the doctor she blamed the prisonlike atmosphere, but as the years went by she began to wonder whether she hadn't subconsciously exaggerated the horrors in order to disguise the real reason she had brought her mother home: the fact that she still needed her, needed her just as long as there was even the remotest possibility she might become well enough to resemble the strong, supportive mother Elaine vaguely remembered from her earliest childhood—and missed.

She would have long black hair, worn loose over her shoulders; hands that were as soft and smooth as a baby's; curious eyes that contrasted oddly with a placid mouth, as if she were always asking a question but never caring whether it was answered. This image

27

had actually existed once upon a time, but so long ago that Elaine couldn't be sure that it was her mother she was remembering or a picture of her mother, taken before Elaine was born and lost before she could differentiate the memories.

Even now, there were traces left of the younger version—her mother's hands were still soft and perfectly smooth; her gray hair was still lustrous. It was the eyes and mouth that had changed over the years, placidity and curiosity switching positions, until now it was her lips that were querulous and pouting, her eyes that were impassive and dull.

They went through a well-synchronized routine on Sundays. When Elaine first opened her eyes, her mother would be sitting on the end of her bed, dressed in the same blue suit she'd worn since the forties, her hands folded demurely on her lap like a little girl determined to be good. Elaine would get up and plug the coffee in, dash back to the bedroom for her jeans, turn the thermostat higher, wrap her mother up in her old fur coat and take her to church. Take her, that is, downstairs to the workshop, sit her down on a wooden bench near the bookcase, hand her a quarter for collection, watch her nod without really hearing, see her push herself up to attention for the Doxology. Elaine would quickly lock the door behind her and drive down to the avenue for the paper and some buns, hurrying back in time to take her mother out to a restaurant called Miller's Hash Heaven she'd been going to ever since she was a girl. Take her, that is, into the kitchen, sit her down at the table, listen to her explain how fine the choir had sounded that morning, hear her describe all the people she could see promenading by the Miller window dressed in their Sunday best.

"Oh, there's Florence Peterson!" she'd say, waving frantically toward the refrigerator. "I must remember to ask her how Lydia made out at Sunday school. You will remind me, won't you, Elaine?"

"Yes, Mommy. Lydia in Sunday School. She's been dead twenty-three years, Mommy."

"What did you say?"

"Nothing, Mommy. Be a good girl now and eat your corn."

Her mother would gather a forkful ever so carefully from her plate, then forget why an inch or two before the fork managed to reach her mouth. The kernels dribbled back down on the tablecloth, and Elaine would have to remind her to start all over again.

"Quick, Elaine! Over there by the hydrant! There's Mabel. Mabel! Over here, Mabel!"

"Mabel died of cancer, Mommy. It was in her liver."

"Why do you mumble so, Elaine? You're sounding more and more like your father every day."

"The corn, Mommy. It's good for you."

After lunch they would sit in the darkened living room watching what few home movies were left after the fire, Elaine behind the projector, her mother on the couch, wheezing the way she always did after a big meal, waving her wrist toward the screen whenever she spotted something she liked. This wasn't often now. More and more she seemed to find the images disturbing. She would get up and go over to the screen, pressing her face against the picture, rubbing the palm of her hand over the warm, pebbly surface as if searching for someone who wasn't there.

"What's wrong, Mommy? Can't you see?"

"I can see perfectly well, thank you."

"Then why don't you sit down over here?"

"Why yes. Yes, I think I will. You're such a thoughtful girl, Elaine. It's a shame you never found anyone to marry. There was that nice Michael you used to go to the movies with."

"Yes, Mommy. Michael was a queer. He liked to whisper to little boys in the rest room during intermission."

"Michael would have been a good son to me. Are there any more films, love?"

The movies were old; they had never been able to afford a decent camera, and over the years a white gap had appeared in the middle of the film where the coating had worn off. There was nothing on most of them any more except a rectangular blank bordered by various hands and feet. Elaine had seen them so many times that she had come to think of her own past in the same way. She was like a partially blind person who could see perfectly well on the sides but nothing at all toward the center. Half her mother. Two interrupted thirds of her father. Wing-tipped shoes of uncles who had died before she knew them. White-gloved hands of deceased maiden aunts. Even her dreams were like that now. Dreams with their middles ripped out, missing people evaporating into widening white holes before she could identify them.

It bothered her. It bothered her because there were no missing centers in other people's films—they were so overendowed with relatives and friends one or two less wouldn't matter. As a beginner, she had often had trouble making good splices and would occasionally accidentally cut away a relative or two before getting it right. At first this clumsiness terrified her. "Mr. Smith," she'd say, rehearsing her apology before picking up the phone, "I'm terribly sorry but I just lost your Uncle Bill." But the odd thing was that people never noticed. A missing cousin, a missing boy friend . . . what difference did it make when there were cousins and boy friends to spare? Her workshop floor was covered with scraps of people she had sacrificed for better splices. There were so many leftovers, in fact, that she had often thought of borrowing them to use in patching up her own films, much the way a movie director brings on extras, inconsequential in themselves, to fill in the empty spaces around his stars. God knows the films needed something. Her mother was getting awfully choppy in the older ones. Reinforcements of fresh film would make her run that much more smoothly through the projector. As it was, if you subtracted one pale hand, eliminated one brown foot, the films would have been entirely blank . . . blank like her dreams, an empty stream of rushing white life on which nothing and no one had ever registered.

There was another category to add to this list of missing persons, one that bothered her even more.

For as long as she could remember, Elaine had had a deep, secret sympathy for anyone born in the late winter or early spring of 1946; born, in other words, nine months after the Second World War had come to an end. To her, the babies born within this interval would always be her own generation, one that was so special and promising it had little in common with children born later that summer or fall, let alone the following year. When she met people who looked the proper age, she would find an excuse to ask their exact birth date, much as an astrologer would, convinced in the same irrational way that the starting point in their lives meant everything. She had even got so she could recognize such people without asking—at airports, sitting across the aisle from her at the theater, passing hurriedly by on the street. It was an intuition she had, the empathetic knowledge that exists between twins.

It got in the way occasionally. She had never been willing to date men her own age in college, for instance, finding that she knew them so well that such a relationship seemed oddly incestuous. She could never explain this to them and they would always go away angry, leaving her with an unrequited fraternal feeling that was as strong in its way as the sexual interest they failed to arouse. It was the same even now. Remembering them, she would feel a combination of emotions difficult to describe—the happiness a baby might feel surrounded by other babies in a small, comfortably heated room; the sadness and nostalgia a veteran might feel reading about fellow soldiers who had fallen upon hard times.

And, of course, some of them had fallen upon hard times. Some were already dead, others were leading pathetic, inconsequential lives they hated. But she knew there was one essential fact about them that could never be taken away: *They started at the same time Elaine had, from the same impulse and gesture—two people long separated rushing into each other's arms, each amazed to find the other was still alive.*

Two people. A soldier on a troopship returning to New York, his wife somewhere down below with his parents on the pier. Confusion, missing faces, 15,000 GI's on the ship, 30,000 civilians on the pier, confetti, horns, cameras, laughing, crying even before the ship docked. The wounded are unloaded first. They smile, they wave. One is helped out of his wheelchair by a pretty nurse who holds him steady while he bends down to kiss the ground . . . Is he wounded, she wonders, pressing closer to the fence. Will she remember me, he asks, elbowing himself to a spot nearer the rail. An instant more of confusion. The soldier steps onto the gangplank leading down to the pier, with his barracks bag slung over one shoulder; his wife separates herself from the crowd near the exit, and then, in every old newsreel Elaine had ever watched, every documentary, every photo, the wife runs across the pier to the bottom of the gangway just in time to be lifted off her feet into her husband's arms, the two of them alone in the enveloping crowd, as if nothing and no one will ever make them let go.

Two people . . . A German soldier coming back to his village to find his wife over a fire in what is left of their small home. He knocks on the door like a stranger, even though the door is open. She stares at him for a moment without recognizing who it is, then bursts into tears . . . A Polish Jew searching for his fiancée among the refugee camps of Austria. Giving up, then months later finding her cutting grass in a meadow near a farm where he has gone to look for work. Standing there on the muddy shoulder of the road too frightened to move, patting down his hair with spit the same way he had when first calling at her parents' home in Warsaw seven years before . . . A teenage girl in London waiting outside her flat morning after morning, convinced he'll appear up the street from the river. Finally, with no word, unable to stand the suspense any longer, she takes the day off from work and goes to Victoria Station to wait there. Through some miracle she is standing on the correct platform when her husband is the first to step off the very next troop train that arrives. So tightly is she hugging him, so tightly is he hugging her, that it isn't until they reach the street that she notices that his left sleeve is tied with a piece of string to his belt.

Two people. Japanese, Russian, French. Two people together again after long years apart. Together after giving each other up for dead. Together in what Elaine always imagined was a sudden hush punctuated by the call of small birds, as if a long-postponed spring had finally arrived.

Nine months later, at the start of another spring, Elaine's generation had its start. Love babies, not war babies—a perfect consummation of love and longing that could result in only the most star-blessed of babies, each of whom would be beautiful, each of whom would be strong. Babies fussed over as no future brothers or sisters would ever be, babies to be petted and indulged no matter what their misdeeds. The children that followed in the next four years—Elaine would admit some similarities with those born through 1949; those born in 1950 might as well have been Martians—came from other gestures: a feeling of obligation, a moment of passion in an otherwise commonplace day. In growing up they couldn't possibly know the same feeling of identity Elaine's contemporaries had. She felt she could describe a whole series of experiences that were theirs and theirs alone, from the first day of kindergarten (the children cry more than usual because they've been spoiled more than usual; the teacher has to let them make paper rabbits even though she had been saving paper rabbits for their second day), through the fifties (Korea, of course, but who cares except Elaine and even she cries in private, realizing by now that she is entered upon a race toward the future and she mustn't let the other runners get too far ahead), through high school, through college, all the way to the mid-sixties, the late fall of 1966 in Boston, when, for reasons she was never afterward sure of, she somehow lost sight of the other children, as suddenly and completely as if a hole had unexpectedly opened beneath her feet.

That December her mother was seriously ill for the first time. Elaine left school for a semester, and when she got back her class had already graduated. The students she met now were a year or two younger than she was, or a year or two older. It was as though everyone her exact age had been banished. Magazines had started using the phrase "generation gap" that year; to Elaine this was something that existed between people who were born in 1946 and those born in 1947. She began to long to meet someone her own age, convinced that no one else could possibly understand her. In the self-pitying moods she was prone to that spring, she would picture herself as the missing person, imagining all her old classmates gathered together somewhere in secret, pursuing a marvellous goal they were very close to now and would soon achieve without her. At other times she would think of them as the ones who had vanished, an entire generation lost, *physically* lost, not lost in some vague literary sense. What had happened to them? Where were they? She worried about them as the survivor of an air crash in the jungle worries about those she leaves behind when she goes for help. It was up to her to rescue them. It was up to her to find out where they had gone.

The autumn before her mother got sick, Elaine had been sitting on a bench on Boston Common, waiting for a friend to meet her for lunch. It was November, and although it was still early, the air had the twilight quality of a late summer evening. Below her, across an empty lawn, was a walkway running along the far edge of the park. It slanted very gradually downhill. Whether it was because of the intervening shrubbery or some blotting, absorbent quality in the sunlight, she couldn't see where it started or ended. As she sat there watching, a line of people came in sight, walking slowly from right to left. There were little boys dribbling half-inflated soccer balls, old ladies with shopping bags, a pair of lovers strolling hand in hand. It was all very stately, all very still. There was a gap of several minutes between strollers, and this gave the scene a processional quality. People appeared, people passed, people faded away. In the silence, she became puzzled. Where were they disappearing to? At the same time she felt she knew, or at least *should* know, even though she couldn't see. And then the answer suddenly occurred to her, occurred to her so forcefully that there could be no doubt. They were walking into the past. Walking into it actually, not metaphorically. The end of the walkway led into a hole in the earth which everyone knew was there but didn't talk about or worry over—right here in the center of Boston was the ramp down which people disappeared into the past.

The more the years went by, the more she realized that this was where her generation had gone. Not toward the future. Not ahead of her any more, but behind her in the years gone by. If she still wanted to find them, she would have to get on that walkway herself and hurry after them like Alice down the rabbit hole. There was no other cure. She was running out of time. The feeling of loss had begun to dominate her dreams to the exclusion of all else, manifesting itself as a white gap like the blanks in their home movies, only whiter, emptier, without even those disembodied hands and feet to indicate that someone actually had been there.

3

Elaine didn't believe in making house calls. There was her mother to worry about for one thing—she always tried to escape if she was left alone for any length of time. There was the sheer bother of it for another—her clients were too widely scattered to make deliveries feasible. And if she did sometimes go to their apartments, it was usually next to impossible to get away. She would hand them the completed past thing through the door, wait there in the hall while they wrote out a check, be on the point of leaving, when they would suddenly remember something else they wanted patched as well. They would drag her inside and sit her down while they rummaged through the closets, ending up keeping her there the entire afternoon, appraising old post-card collections, leafing through peeling finger paintings their youngest daughter had made in first grade.

There was only one exception: Major Haig-Brown. He didn't live as far away as the others—Elaine could easily walk it on a nice day. With his leg and his bad eye, it would have been impossible for him to come to her. Then, too, he wasn't as demanding as most of her clients. He knew how hard it was to repair the past, and he was brave and honest enough to be content with having what few souvenirs he still had merely fixed. *Fixed,* not enhanced. Polish on something that hadn't been shiny even when brand new, letting out the waist on an old uniform so it would fit . . . none of this was for him. He had more past than most of her clients but made fewer demands on it; he didn't cheat. No nostalgia for nostalgia's sake, no embarrassing sentiment. Major Haig-Brown believed in seeing things the way they were.

He was a special man in several respects. Elaine had been half in love with him for the past two years.

Half in love. She always qualified it this way. Half in love, like a schoolgirl who has a crush on her favorite teacher but is sensible enough, even at thirteen, to know anything more is out of the question. And even the half Elaine was willing to admit was directed less toward the Major Haig-Brown of the present than toward the Lieutenant Haig-Brown of sixty years ago—the shy, boyish-looking officer staring out at her from sepia photographs taken in England in 1914, the oval miniatures done in France the following year. Both revealed a remarkably gentle face—a face that, with its innocent confidence, you couldn't imagine existing much beyond that last summer before the war. With it came all the associations of life as it had been at its most Edwardian: the fragile women in high-necked dresses serving tea; punts on the sun-swirled Thames; young men at eighteen posing under a heartbreakingly blue blue sky; the remarkable flawless beauty of a perfect July, all of which—fragile women, confident men, flawless sky—was doomed, though no one knew it.

This was the part she was half in love with. The illusion—the myth. And as in all good half-love affairs, there was jealousy involved, too. Her name was Catherine. She was the twin to the sepia miniature—the sixteen-year-old daughter of the parish vicar in the Wiltshire village where the major grew up. That was all Elaine really knew about her. Her name was Catherine, she was very young, very beautiful, and Major Haig-Brown had once loved her more than any other person in the world.

She had often wondered what had happened to end it. The major moved to America after the war, moved there alone and never visited England again. Too drafty, he would say when she asked him. Too bloody cold. But it was obvious from the way he brushed her questions aside that there were deeper reasons, too. Elaine's own theory was that he had crammed too much experience, good and bad, into his first twenty years, that returning home after all he had suffered would have been too anticlimactic. This, coupled with the heartbreak she instinctively knew he must in some way have gone through with Catherine, might have forced him to find somewhere new where he could start over again, without the burden of remembering that far-off July.

But, of course, this was pure guesswork on her part. He seldom spoke about his life prior to coming to the States, at least not with her. He had become an ardent baseball fan during his years in New York, and most of the time they ended up talking about how the local teams were doing, instead of the vanished lives and lost loves Elaine longed to ask him about. He would get out his yearbook to look up batting averages, she would pretend to be interested, and they would end up talking baseball the entire afternoon, Elaine feeling bored and ashamed of herself for not being honest.

The problem was she wanted so much to be as young and innocent for him as his oldest past things were; wanted him to judge her—*approve* her—by the same standards he had used in choosing a sweetheart sixty years before; wanted, no matter how silly she told herself it was, to compete with Catherine for whatever pulse of emotion lingered on from that young lieutenant's love. She was always terribly nervous before she visited him. She would adjust her hair time and time again (up was best, up looked suitably demure), would change into dress after dress until she found one that might possibly be old-fashioned enough to please him. But somehow it never worked. There was always a bit too much make-up on her eyebrows, or a line across her forehead that she couldn't smooth away with cream. She would glance at herself in the mirror, look down at Catherine's miniature, and feel jaded in comparison. She was never quite sure whether it was because she was thirty-five, not sixteen, or because it was the 1980s, and innocence was lost to everyone, not just to her.

＊　＊　＊

She went to see him the day before she was to have lunch with Mr. Powers. As usual, the major didn't hear the bell. As usual, Elaine had to ring three times before his landlady came to the door.

"Yes?" she said, peeking out from behind the screen as if she were expecting muggers. "Who's there, please?"

"It's me, Olga. Elaine Collier."

"Well, why didn't you say so? Come in, come in. Don't be such a stranger."

It was the same routine they always went through.

"How is he today?" Elaine asked.

"The general? Not so good. He's coughing all the time now. I don't like the sound of it these days. The other morning he left the gas on by mistake. If I hadn't gone upstairs to bring him his orange, it would have been good-by general."

"Is he taking medication?"

Olga shrugged. "You know these old army men. You can't tell them nothing. But ask him. Say hello to Katya for a second, then you can go upstairs."

Elaine enjoyed this part of it: scratching the cat behind the ear, admiring the newest plants, listening to stories about who was up to what in the neighborhood. She liked Olga very much. There was something about her that hinted at an important past, and Elaine, for all the fatigue she was feeling lately toward *any* past, wasn't blasé enough not to be interested. Something significant had once happened to Olga. Elaine could see it in the teasing, half-cynical way she joked, the affection she poured out on her cat, the determined way she went about being happy over small things, like someone for whom small things had almost come to an end.

"Tell me, Elaine, how is your mother? Better I hope."

"About the same. She has her good days and her bad."

Olga shook her head sympathetically. "And your business? How is it going with stocks so bad, everyone underemployed?"

"Fairly well, Olga. It can seem monotonous at times just like any other job, of course. I'm at the point right now where I need a challenge. There's a job I have that might be interesting, but I won't know for sure until tomorrow."

Katya was rubbing against her shoe, demanding another scratch. Olga cleared her throat and coughed a pretend cough. She was fidgety in a way Elaine had never seen her before. She suddenly excused herself—to check something on the stove she said. "You wait a minute for me, please."

She came back almost immediately. "I know you told me already, Elaine, but tell me again. What is it exactly you do with yourself?"

Elaine laughed. "I patch up the past, Olga. I mend old things."

"You mean, if I knew someone who had something old they wanted fixed, you could fix it?"

"I could try."

"Even fabric?"

"Even fabric."

"You could fix it up so somebody looking at it could maybe remember better?"

"Yes, Olga."

"How much does it cost? For my friend, I mean."

"That depends."

Olga threw her hands up in the air. "Oh, you businessmen! All the time with your 'depends'! I can see you are one tough cookie to deal with, Mr. Businessman. Go on upstairs and see the general."

They went into the hall. Elaine didn't want to go upstairs unannounced, but the major was hard of hearing so there was no use trying the bell again.

"Just go up," Olga said. "He'll be happy to see you. He maybe is sick, but he still likes pretty girls."

"Then he's in for a disappointment."

"Baloney! You look very nice today, Elaine. You never looked so nice and young before."

"You tell that to all his girls, Olga."

"Well, maybe I do, maybe I don't. You go up there and say hello. In an hour I put the coffee on. You come down here when you're done, we'll talk."

Elaine started up the stairs. They were steep. When she got halfway up, she stopped to catch her breath.

"Major Haig-Brown?" she called.

No one answered.

"Major?"

She hesitated. There was no telling how she might find him, and she worried about the effect surprise could have on his heart.

"Major Haig-Brown? It's me, Elaine Collier."

He wasn't in the kitchen. She checked to make sure the gas was turned off, then went into the small, furniture-stuffed pantry he called his living room.

"I've brought your things, Major."

He wasn't there either. Elaine was wondering whether or not to call down to Olga when she spotted him out on the glass-enclosed adjunct to the living room, which served as his porch. He was sitting in a high-backed chair, facing the street. The back of his head managed to catch what little sunlight filtered through the window—it made her think of a very old, very gray piece of melon.

"How are you feeling, Major?"

No response. She started through the living room, deliberately clicking her heels on the bare spots in the carpeting so he would hear her coming.

"How are you today?" she asked a bit louder.

He didn't move.

"I've brought your things," she said.

She sat down across from him on a footrest near the TV. His eyes were closed, and he seemed to be asleep, but Elaine wasn't sure. He might have been simply resting his eyes. His nose had gone tight and shiny in the way of an old man's, his chin quivered when he inhaled, and it had obviously been several days since he last shaved. On his forehead were five separate diagonal lines running up from his left eye toward his hair. Old battle scars, she assumed. Narrow scoops, like the tracks a small sea animal might leave wiggling across damp sand.

In general, however, the years had treated him lightly. His face wore the gentle, naïve expression of the old photographs. His eyes, now that they were practically blind, had taken on a quality of soft acceptance. His hands had become white and oddly feminine. When Elaine, sitting down, accidentally cut off the sunlight, he brushed them along his cheek as if trying to regather the beams.

"Hello, Major."

"Hello, Elaine."

Had he known she was there all along? He didn't act a bit surprised. Had he been dreaming of her? Of someone who looked like her? There was no hesitation when he opened his eyes. The transition from whatever he had been thinking of to what he was seeing was very smooth.

"I've brought your things."

"I know. Let's take them into the living room, shall we?"

They always spoke this way with each other. No preliminaries, no small talk, as if neither had the inclination to waste breath.

She took out the map first. It was mud-stained, and there had been rips along the edges. She unfolded it across the major's card table so that he could study it in the light.

"It's perfect, Elaine!"

"Do you really think so? I wasn't sure if you still wanted the mud."

The major smiled. "Oh, we must have the mud. I remember

the men saying it was so thick it would never come off. And see here, they were right!"

"It was starting to flake. I kept it in a closet with a humidifier. I thickened some of these lines over here . . ."

"German second trench."

"Their second trench. I wasn't sure if it was important."

"Important enough that ten thousand young men died trying to take it."

Elaine wasn't sure how to answer that. "It's such a small line," she said, reaching into her briefcase for his holster. "I put some polish on this, but just a bit. Just so the leather wouldn't crack."

"Thank you, Elaine. You're simply a magician."

"Does it fit?"

The major's face reddened. "Well, it may be a shade too tight. If I remember, though, it was snug even then. I was so proud to have one I simply couldn't bring myself to take it off. Slept with it actually."

This was what she liked about the major. Most clients would force on her boring descriptions of the events surrounding each past thing in turn, as though she was the audience in some adult version of "Show and Tell." Not the major. He was content with a brief comment on each one, like a poet for whom a simple adjective suffices to sum up an entire world. But the odd thing was that in his case Elaine would have *enjoyed* hearing more, and she couldn't help feeling disappointed when he put the holster aside without a story.

"I believe you must have one more for me, Elaine."

She had saved Catherine's miniature for last. She took it out now and handed it to him across the table, anxious to see what his reaction would be. At first he pretended not to be interested. He put it face down near the holster as if it were merely another wartime souvenir. But finally the temptation was too much for him. He couldn't keep up the bluff any longer.

"Excuse me, Elaine."

43

He took it over to the window where the light was better and held it up near his one good eye like a jewler appraising a rare stone. He had a coughing spell while he was there. His whole body shook, and for a moment Elaine was afraid he'd drop it. But he finally regained possession of himself, came back to the table and sat down as if nothing had happened.

"She was very beautiful," Elaine said.

"You've done wonders with her."

"There was that little scar on the side . . ."

"Shrapnel. One of those bothersome trench mortars they used. Saved my life actually. Had it in my breast pocket at the time. What you might call a bit of good luck."

It was more than she had ever gotten from him before. She probed very gently now, careful not to scare him off by being too abrupt.

"I was wondering what color hair?"

"Red. When I said good-by to her that last time, a strand was caught on my overcoat. Didn't find it until Calais. All the way back to the battalion I remember holding it coiled round my finger like a ring."

"You must have been very fond of her."

The moment she said it, she bit her tongue. The major got up from his chair pretending not to have heard her.

"The time has come," he said, exaggerating his accent the way he did when he felt she was becoming too inquisitive, "for you and me to partake of our afternoon tea, what?"

"Will you take my arm?"

"If you take mine. *Après vous, mademoiselle.*"

He seemed to have a different attitude for every room. Once inside the kitchen, he became clumsy in the best tradition of fussy old men—the various faucets, sockets and dials seemed to confuse him hopelessly. Elaine sat on a stool near the counter as she always did. Except for pouring the tea when it was ready, she wasn't allowed to help. But at least the kitchen was bright and contemporary enough to free another topic of conversation. For the first time since she had known him he told her what it was he had done for a living once he moved to America.

"Public relations, actually. For a hotel chain."

"Do you miss it?"

"Well, only . . . Damn!"

As usual, he had burned his finger on the teapot. Elaine found some butter in the refrigerator and helped him rub it on. They drank their tea without saying much. The major seemed embarrassed. When Elaine was done, she took her cup and rinsed it out in the sink, then glanced down at her watch.

"It's that time again, Major."

He didn't say anything. He was staring down at his saucer as though he hadn't heard.

"I'm afraid I've got to be getting home."

"There's something else," he whispered.

"I'm sorry?"

"There's something I have for you. In my bedroom."

"Something you want patched."

He nodded, keeping his one good eye fixed on the tea. "I'd like you to have it actually. It's in my bedroom."

"May I use your bathroom first?"

The major showed her the way down the hall. It was an old man's bathroom. The back of the toilet was piled with an assortment of rubbing lotions and powders, the medicine cabinet overflowed with prescription bottles needing to be refilled, and there was a heavy smell of damp towels. Elaine combed her hair in the mirror, then tried to straighten things up as best she could.

"Are you all right, Elaine?"

"Be out in a second!"

She finished cleaning off the mirror before she joined him in the bedroom. He was sitting on the edge of the bed with a cookie tin on his lap, like a little boy about to show her his pet frog. Inside was a brittle piece of something that, from where she stood looking down at it, appeared to be old chocolate. The major made her sit down on the bed next to him, then carefully, ever so carefully, handed her the tin.

"I've been saving this for last."

It wasn't chocolate. Up close it looked more like old leather. Old leather or straw.

"Give up?"

"A knife sheath?"

"A flower. Oh, don't ask me what kind. By the time I got it away from him it was pretty well tattered."

It could have been a flower. Stuck to the tin's side was a parchment-colored flake that might possibly once have been a leaf. Across the bottom were bits of dusty puff which, several incarnations ago, could conceivably have formed a blossom. It could have been the dehydrated kind of flower people press between encyclopedia pages and forget.

"It grew on the Somme," the major explained. "It was the first flower to bloom in no man's land when the battle was over."

"You picked it?"

"Not me. Someone else. I suppose I was the first to spot it though. At dawn. We'd have the men stand to in case the Germans were coming across. Used to look things over with the periscope to make sure. I remember because Fitzgerald was still alive at the time. 'Come over here, Bill,' I said. 'Tell me what you make of this.' He saw it straight away. We both saw it. This little pink blossom stretching up out of the mud the other side of our wire."

He had taken the tin back on his lap now. Every so often he dipped his head toward it as though it were a vaporizer, as though he was trying to recapture the blossom's scent.

"We didn't get it, of course. Not that first time. Daft of me even to try. But, you see, we hadn't been out there very long, so we still had these rather chivalrous notions about how things stood. Wanted to prove ourselves I suppose. Sweetheart at home I wanted it for, that kind of thing."

"Catherine?"

The major nodded. "Germans beat us to it actually. Ran smack into them. The funny thing is they must have been new men, too. The moment we saw one another, they ran away just as fast as we did. I remember Bill saying he hadn't seen speed like that since his last Derby. That night I went out myself, but of course it was too dark by then. Couldn't find the bloody thing. Next morning I felt wretched, risking lives on it. But there it was, you see, I couldn't take my eyes off it. All that week in fact. Kept getting bigger and bigger. Doing quite well actually. All that moisture in the ground. I remember letting the men take turns looking through my glass at it. 'Bit of 'ome,' they'd say. And what was so odd, I knew Jerry was doing the same thing. There was this lieutenant of theirs. I'd spotted him when we stumbled into their patrol. Big handlebar mustache. Field cap, no helmet. I knew he wanted it even more than I did because now and again we'd see his cap peeking over their sandbags at it. Taking chances. Asking for a bullet. I suppose he was the only man left in France who was as romantic as I was, poor bastard."

Elaine could hear Olga moving around the kitchen downstairs. The sound seemed to disturb the major. He got up from the bed and limped back and forth near the window.

"I simply *had* to get it. After a while I convinced Bill to go out with me. Waited for a foggy morning. I remember because it was the first time either of us had ever been over the top in daylight standing up. We'd taken a sight on the flower before we left, so there was no trouble finding it. Only as it turned out we were too late. The German lieutenant had gotten there ahead of us. He looked up and saw us just as he was sticking the flower in his cap."

Downstairs, Olga dropped a pot. The major stopped next to the window and stood there looking down at the street.

"What happened then?" Elaine asked softly.

No answer.

"What happened then?"

The major came back to the bed.

"The other day I was looking at it when this fell out. It's a seed of some kind, isn't it?"

He dipped his hand into the tin and brought out something that resembled a small ebony pebble. He wiped it off carefully on his shirt and handed it to Elaine.

"I'd like you to take it home with you and see if it will grow."

"I can't," Elaine said automatically.

"I'd try myself, but I'm afraid I'm not much good with plants."

"Neither am I. They make me sneeze."

It was a foolish thing to say. She could tell he was serious about it—he'd probably been awake half the night trying to get up the nerve to ask her.

"See how dry it is," she said. "It can't possibly grow after all these years."

The major shrugged. "I suppose you're right. But do you think you might give it a go? It would mean a lot to me to see it again. See the actual flower of it I mean. I've kept it all this time. Never sure why actually. Thought of giving it to a museum when I die. Somewhere they could take proper care of it . . . The Unknown Flower, don't you know? It must be a very special one to have grown there in the mud where everything else died."

"Maybe it's a poppy," Elaine suggested.

"Maybe. I thought if we could get it to grow again we could find out. I had one miracle already there in the trenches, Elaine. I remember promising myself I'd never ask for another. But now I am asking. I am asking you, Elaine."

She took it, of course. The major wrapped it up in layers of toilet paper for her, like someone swaddling a mummy. He had another coughing spell before she left, this one much worse than before. She sat with him until he was feeling well enough to accompany her to the top of the stairs.

"I want to thank you for all you've done," he said.

She had gotten up the nerve now. She was finally going to ask him about Catherine, what had happened to them, but before she could he did something that surprised her and made her stop. He reached out and put his hand against her cheek.

"You're such a pretty girl, you know."

"Thank you," Elaine said, taken aback.

It was very quiet there in the hall. The sun had gone down. She could hardly see him in the dark.

"I'm going to miss you terribly," he said, his hand sliding down her hair until it came to rest on her shoulder. "I want to remember you exactly like this. You're so beautiful."

His hand was around her waist. He started pulling her very gently toward him. Elaine closed her eyes. She was trying very hard to concentrate on the pictures she'd seen of him when he was young, trying to force twenty years off her own life until she would seem just as chaste and innocent as the girl she knew he saw there before him.

"I want you to be good while I'm away."

"I will," Elaine said. "I promise."

Was this her reward? Was this what she had earned by flirting so obviously with the past? To be taken there? Between one heartbeat and the next, taken back to a train station somewhere, to a last moment together before the train pulled away?

"Goodbye. I . . . I love you," he stammered. Then he kissed her, Elaine standing very still, as if she had never really been kissed before. It was the lightest brush against her lips, the way a boy would kiss a girl he loved too much to hold tighter. The last faint, lingering vestige of an overpowering emotion spent sixty years before.

"So how was he already?" Olga asked. "Still all the time playing Romeo?"

She wasn't ready for Mr. Powers when he came. In order to get her mother to take her nap early, she had moved the day's schedule up, giving her breakfast at seven instead of eight, lunch at eleven-thirty rather than one. Elaine peeled an orange for her dessert, then, when she showed no sign of getting sleepy, went into the bedroom to get dressed. By the time she got back, her mother was gone.

"Dear Elaine," the note on the refrigerator door said, "I'm going to see the Dodgers at Ebbet's Field. I'll be back for dinner. Your loving Mother."

Elaine checked to see that she was really sleeping, then went into the bathroom to fix her hair, wondering why she was taking such pains over an interview she was determined to keep as short as possible.

She hadn't come up with any answers by the time the doorbell rang. Her hair wasn't quite combed the way she wanted it, and the excitement she felt at the prospect of seeing him hadn't lasted long enough for her to give it definition. The only part of her preparations she was satisfied with were John's things, wrapped in brown paper on her desk ready to give back to him, the top folds left untaped so there could be no mistaking what the package contained.

"Hello, Miss Collier."

"Hello, Mr. Powers."

As she had planned, he followed her through the hall to her office. As she had planned, he immediately caught sight of the package and stopped short.

"What's this?" he said finally, frowning.

"I told you it was a waste of time," Elaine said, reciting the lines she had rehearsed in the bathroom. "I was packing them up when the doorbell rang."

Mr. Powers stared down at John's graduation picture. Elaine expected him to start arguing with her, but he only stood there, running one finger along the frame.

Finally, the silence was too much for her.

"I don't think I'll have the time for him."

"So you said." Mr. Powers did not look up.

"Mysteries aren't really in my line."

"It's not a mystery."

"What is it then?"

But the moment by her desk had apparently been long enough for him to regain his self-possession. When he turned back to her, he was smiling as if nothing were wrong.

"Let's go somewhere for lunch."

"Lunch?"

Elaine couldn't have been more startled if he had suddenly asked her to bed.

"Would you mind? I think it would be easier to explain in a more relaxed setting."

"I can't leave my mother alone for very long."

"I promise to have you back no later than two. You didn't get dressed so nicely just to stay here, did you?"

"I'm going out later."

"Oh." It was difficult to tell whether or not he believed her. "Well, in that case, we better get going. Will your hair stand it if I put the top down? It's a lovely day."

Everything happened so fast that Elaine didn't have time to think about it. She hurried upstairs to check on her mother, rummaged through the dresser for a scarf, hurried back downstairs again to turn on the phone-answering machine and take a few hopeless swipes with the brush at her hair. By the time she got outside, Mr. Powers was holding open the door of his sports car for her. He rested his hand lightly on her back as she slid in.

A buzzer sounded on the dashboard. Mr. Powers had to reach over and buckle her seat belt for her before it went off.

"It's been ages since I've ridden in a Corvette," Elaine explained, feeling awkward.

"Actually, it's a Jaguar. All set?"

"There's a diner down the street. They have specials for lunch that are pretty good."

Mr. Powers laughed. "Oh, I think we can do a bit better than that," he said.

During the ride Elaine had the same sense of not being adequately prepared that she'd had when he rang the doorbell. She decided it wasn't so much her hair as it was the tremendous gulf that existed between Mr. Powers's world and the major's. The interval between seeing each of them had been too short. She felt as though she had been wrenched back from a decade where she was expected to be demure and innocent to a decade where she was expected to be knowing and chic, and she wasn't sure she could bring it off.

"Is it far?" she asked, seeing a sign for the Expressway.

"Not far at all."

Elaine lost her bearings as soon as they left Queens. She supposed they were somewhere on the North Shore near the Sound, but she was too embarrassed to ask. The restaurant turned out to be a Colonial-style inn next to a park. The maître-d' came out in person to welcome them and led them past the dining room to a smaller, more intimate room that overlooked a garden.

"Is this satisfactory, Mr. Powers?" he asked, gesturing for a waiter.

"Fine, Thomas. I've been raving about the clam pie all the way out here. Is it available today?"

"Of course, Mr. Powers. And the young lady?"

"I think we'll let her study your menu first, Thomas. But this table is perfect, thank you."

Elaine had hardly sat down before a waiter arrived. She stared frantically at the menu, then pointed in desperation to the first line.

"I'll have this," she said.

The waiter made a face.

"Would you care for a drink first?" Mr. Powers said tactfully.

"Oh yes. I'll have . . . I'll have whatever you're having."

"Two Manhattans up, Peter."

There was a fireplace in the wall behind their table. A woman dressed in Colonial costume put another log on it, then carried a basket of popovers around to each table.

"Do you like it?" Mr. Powers asked.

Elaine nodded. "I've never been in a place like this. Not in years anyway. Are you sure this is still Long Island? I feel we're in a different world."

Mr. Powers seemed very concerned with putting her at her ease. He asked her what kind of wine she liked ("Oh, any old kind," Elaine said), what kind of music and plays. All the while they talked, he fingered a pen he had taken from his jacket pocket, giving Elaine the curious feeling that he was interviewing her— that she was being gently, subtly probed.

He kept up the flow of small talk during cocktails, brought the conversation around to his wife during appetizers, and got to his main point just as the waiter brought their entreés.

"I think I underestimated the tenacity of Carol's memory," he began.

"In what way?"

"I thought that if I could just find a way of getting John's things out of the house, it would be less painful for her after a while. It's the reason I talked her into seeing you."

"And why you told me there was no hurry?"

"Yes. I apologize for not being more frank. Am I forgiven?"

"I suppose so."

He poured her a glass of wine.

"It was a bad idea," he admitted. "A good percentage of the things we have are worth preserving. The pictures, for instance. They're from good years mostly, the good years I worked hard for. I don't want to get rid of all our memories, just the ones that torment Carol."

"Memory doesn't work like that, Mr. Powers. It's all or nothing."

He looked skeptical. "Is it?"

The maître d' came over to tell him there was a phone call for him in the lobby. Elaine felt self-conscious sitting alone—she wasn't sure whether to go on eating or wait. Then, too, there was something about the phone call that bothered her.

"Business," he said brusquely, sitting down. "Have you ordered dessert yet?"

Elaine shook her head. "You knew we were coming here, didn't you? The restaurant expected you, and whoever called knew you'd be here, too. You knew I'd say yes all along."

"Let's just say I *hoped* you would. There's a big difference."

He called the waiter over and ordered coffee. "Now, where were we before I left?"

"You were talking about getting rid of your son."

He smiled. "You make it sound so harsh. I'm only doing it for Carol. But yes, that's more or less what I'm asking you to do. Help me make her forget him. Send her back some of his things and keep all the rest. Do it gradually so that she won't miss him. Any picture that has him in, take him out. Take him out of anything you can. Patch up the past *around* him."

"I'm not sure I understand."

"I'll show you." He reached across the table for the wine list, sketched three crude stick figures on its cover with his pen, then carefully ripped it down the middle to separate them. The piece with two figures left on it he gave to Elaine. The smaller piece with the remaining figure he crumpled into a ball in his fist.

"Say you put that in your purse for a souvenir," he said. "Say years from now you take it out to relive old times. You'll only remember the two men you can actually see on the paper, not the third who was once there. Get my point? Memories need evidence to survive. Without it . . ."

"You're asking me to destroy evidence?"

"For a good cause."

"John's the third man?"

"Exactly. Can you do it?"

"It wouldn't be easy," Elaine said carefully.

"But will you?"

"I suppose so. Lot's of people bring me pictures and tell me to crop out relatives they don't like or ex-wives or something. It might even be a challenge."

"I'd be eternally grateful. Carol's been nearly insane since he died. The only thing he's good for now is to torture her."

"But why didn't you tell me all this before? Why all the mystery?"

"I wasn't quite sure how to go about asking you," Mr. Powers said quietly. "It's never been easy for me to admit I need help."

"That's silly. I'm the last person in the world anyone should be shy with."

"I know that now, Elaine. You're a completely different person away from that office of yours. Much more approachable and real."

Elaine felt a flush of pleasure. It was no use pretending to herself that she wasn't tempted by the job. For years she had worked on people like the Shugrues with their cheap pottery and tattered postcards. Perhaps it was time to work for someone else, someone who was part of a completely different existence than the one she had been brought up in, someone to whom good restaurants and expensive wines weren't things to dream about but things to experience and enjoy.

She ran her hand nervously around the top of her coffee cup, trying not to let her eagerness show.

"But assuming I could do it, Mr. Powers, what would I do with your son's things that are left over? It wouldn't seem right just to throw them out."

Mr. Powers shrugged. "That's entirely up to you."

"I'll need more of his things, too."

"I have another box in the car."

"I'll have to know more about him."

"Is that wise? You don't want to get too involved."

"I'm curious about him. Most of the people I work on are in their sixties and seventies, and someone my own age would be a nice change."

Mr. Powers hesitated. "He's not the kind of boy you would get a crush on, is he?"

"He was my own age, Mr. Powers. I never go out with men my own age."

"What kind of men do you go out with?"

He had the pen in his hand again, only he wasn't playing with it this time—he had it poised expectantly between his fingers as if this were the question he had been leading up to all along.

"I don't know. There's been no one in years."

The moment she said it, she regretted it. It was giving him too much of herself, a secret that he hadn't earned. She wasn't sure whether or not he sensed this; his only reaction was to change the subject and smile.

"Well, that means you'll do it then, right?"

"Work on John? I'll *try* it, Mr. Powers. That's all I can promise."

"That's good enough for me . . . Finished?"

He called the waiter over with the check. As he led her past the bar, someone called to him.

"Can you wait here for a second?" he asked. "I'll do a little quick fence-mending and be right back."

There was a business meeting of some sort in progress in the taproom, and whoever it was who had called him over insisted on introducing him to everyone who was there. Elaine watched him move among the small groups near the dais, shaking hands like a candidate working a reception line, squeezing hard for sincerity's sake but sizing up each man, too, calculating exactly what form of appeal it would take to win him over to his side. What was he running for? Elaine wondered. Was there some privilege he hadn't achieved yet? Some prize? Or was it just a lifetime habit he couldn't break—manipulating purely for the satisfaction he found in manipulation? Elaine saw one of the men glance over at her, laugh and slap Mr. Powers on the back. She decided to wait for him in the parking lot.

"I'm sorry I made you wait," he said when he came out.

"Can I ask you one more favor? I'd really like to take home a menu to show my mother. I was too shy to ask the waiter."

Mr. Powers laughed. "One souvenir coming up."

He went into the restaurant again and was back in a minute with a menu. Elaine carefully folded it in half and put it in her pocketbook. An attendant brought the car. Mr. Powers still had the scrap of paper with the drawing in his fist, but once they reached the highway he rolled down the window and tossed it out.

The following morning she began work on John.

It was easier than she had expected, at least at first. John had a habit of standing a bit apart from whomever else he was posing with in a photograph, so it was simply a question of taking a razor to him and making the separation complete: John and his class in kindergarten, John standing alone off to the right near the swings; John and his Little League baseball team, John a good three inches taller than the rest of the boys, his head jutting awkwardly above theirs in the back row as if waiting to be chopped off; John and his friends on the deck of the family boathouse on Martha's Vineyard, John standing aloof on the diving board, staring down at the water as if contemplating a sudden dive out of the camera's view. He always looked that way—on the point of fleeing.

The gap grew wider as he became older. A quarter-inch in the early photos—she had to be careful here, biting her tongue in concentration, bending over the photos until her face almost touched his, trying to avoid slashing the faces of bystanders who were meant to survive—a half-inch in the later ones, a margin of blank film gradually widening between his own handsome figure and the constant, surrounding halo of family and friends. Occasionally some well-intentioned person would try to bridge the gap by reaching out to him at the moment the picture was taken. A beautiful red-headed girl playfully stuck out a tennis racket to pull him closer to the net. A boy his age looped the mainsheet of a sailboat over his head trying to keep him from sliding off the stern. His mother, younger here, with a beauty that was startling, twisted sideways to put her arm around his shoulder just as he ducked. No matter how hard they tried, it was always too late. The picture was shot, their effort blurred—a clumsy attempt to join him to the mainstream that was out of focus from the start.

Elaine remembered what Mr. Powers had said about not becoming too interested in John, and she went about her business with scissors and paste trying to keep her mind on something else. But no matter how hard she tried, she couldn't help wondering about the gap, wondering why it got bigger as he got older, wondering, most of all, what there was in John that corresponded to the separation. She had intended to devote only one day a week to working on him, but on Monday morning she took out his pictures again.

He wasn't shy. There were too many pictures of him with his arm—his *outstretched* arm—around pretty girls for that. He wasn't a loner. There were the teams he had belonged to, the cards of membership from various clubs. He certainly wasn't neglected. Based upon even the most casual examination of the past things Mr. Powers had brought over, it was obvious that John had enjoyed privilege and favor all his life: coaches and teachers who were anxious to further his skills, summer camp in Maine, prep school in New Hampshire, college in Vermont. If there was an ever-present isolation, it seemed to be less a separation caused by some inner rebellion than one thrust upon him by fate, as if life had found him out amid all the protective devices and marked him for a different destiny than that lying in wait for all the other handsome, wealthy adolescents among whom he had grown up.

Besides the photos of John with his friends, there were family pictures to rearrange: the Powers next to their Christmas tree, the Powers at a wedding, the three of them always in the picture together, giving Elaine the impression that they had a permanent cameraman stationed within reach at all times; the Powers in the Caribbean, the Powers in Colorado; John with his diving equipment, John in his climbing boots, still with the same expectant concentration on his face, a bit taller from picture to picture, his forehead starting to take on the same shape as his father's. Elaine always held the razor in her left hand, bringing it carefully along the ink marks she circled around his head, the trailing fingertips of her right hand pressing down the ragged edges the razor would leave, smoothing them, lingering for a moment on the glossy, satinlike features of Mr. Powers who stood there with his arm possessively linked to that of his wife.

By lunchtime she would be left with two little piles: photographs with John still in them; photographs in which John had been removed. It was strange about these last. John's removal didn't seem to make much difference to them. There were no jagged holes where he had been, no tattered edges. If anything, the cropped photos looked *more* natural once he was gone. She pasted them carefully back together, cutting away any stray bits of hair or flesh that were left, patching any tear marks that showed, holding the finished photo to the light to see if there were any portions of him she had missed. The John-less ones she packed away in an envelope to return to Mrs. Powers. The others went into her bottom drawer until she had time to take them out and start the whole process again.

Later in the week a parcel-post van pulled up outside the house with two large packages of things from John's boyhood: teddy bears he'd once gone to sleep with, a BB gun, souvenir pennants from various resorts. Mr. Powers had told her how important it was for his wife to trust her, so Elaine polished up the gun and sent it back to them, but she wasn't sure what to do with all the rest—rusty fishing reels, old fire trucks, sports trophies, scouting badges, local newspapers with his picture in them, small under-lined articles about his latest awards. They filled every spare shelf in her workshop, but she couldn't bring herself to throw them out, not yet, not until she was sure Mrs. Powers wouldn't miss them.

At least the newspapers could be worked on. There were several cartons of them. Apparently Mrs. Powers had saved, besides every newspaper that ever mentioned her son's name, every one pub-lished on a significant date: his birthday, the day he graduated from prep school, the day he went away to college. There must have been more than a hundred in all. Elaine had to leaf through each in turn to make sure his picture wasn't there. If it was, she had to cut it out and replace it with another the same size from one of the John-less editions. John accepting a trophy for being the best tennis player at school was replaced by a picture of a local New Hampshire selectman pinning a blue ribbon on a cow. John accepting the rank of Eagle Scout was replaced by a grinning used-car salesman standing proudly in front of his new lot. After that she juggled the captions, moving headlines, shuffling col-umns to make everything fit—to make sure Mrs. Powers wouldn't notice any holes.

It was difficult work. Sometimes in the middle of her cutting she would get tired and end up reading the front pages instead. The inside of her thumb hurt from the scissors, her eyes were tired . . . she would slump in her chair with a cup of lukewarm tea.

The papers were all from the late fifties and early sixties. Good news mostly. Family, country, home and school. The enemy was well-defined and distant, the disasters mild, scarcely worthy of the name. What crimes there were happened somewhere else; the talk was of surplus this, surplus that, and there was no hint of any shortage of money, confidence or good sense. It was an orderly, reassuring world that smelled vaguely of musty orange.

It seemed strange that John with his unruly hair and questioning frown should blend in so well with these newspapers. There wasn't the inevitable gap there was in the family snapshots. John's picture was indistinguishable from any other on the page. He seemed somehow linked with what was most solid, unchanging and humdrum: John on the same page with a wire story about Eisenhower on vacation in Georgia—John the goalie outstretched in midair stopping a shot, Eisenhower with golf club in hand, wincing as his drive went wide; John above and to the left of advertisements for new housing developments along the Connecticut shore; John accepting a young-man-of-the-year award from the local Rotarians; John on the same page with the interstate highways, the early space shots, the vaccine for measles.

And yet in the end he separated easily from these as well. She didn't even have to use scissors, he simply tore away in her hands. She would be edging her finger along the picture, trying to make a crease she could follow with the razor, when the whole column would tear like tissue. She would be carefully taping a new picture in the empty space where his head had been when the entire page would disintegrate—suddenly, for no reason at all. By the time she was done with the first editions, she was left not with a young man perfectly enmeshed in an affluent, optimistic world, but with dust.

She swept it up and was turning off the workshop lights when the phone rang. It was Mr. Powers.

"Hello, Elaine. Not interrupting anything, am I?"

"Oh, hello. No. No, not at all."

"I just wanted to tell you how much I admired the first batch of pictures you sent up. I could hardly tell where the changes had been made myself."

"Thank you. It's been even more interesting than I thought it would be. I'm still bothered by his leftovers though."

"Leftovers?"

"The pieces of him I've cut out. I feel guilty throwing them away. Are you sure you don't want me to save them for you?"

He didn't respond to this. He went on talking as though he hadn't heard her.

"Are you doing anything the Sunday after next?" he asked. "I thought I'd bring John's school things down, and then we could drive into the city, have lunch, do a museum."

"That sounds lovely, only . . . It's hard for me to get away on Sundays."

"Because of your mother? You mustn't let her tie you down all the time. Can't you find someone to look after her?"

"There's Mrs. Peabody next door. I suppose I could ask her. What time would it be?"

"How does one o'clock sound? In the meantime, I'll be sending you the first few reels of our home movies. Could you do the same thing on them you've done on the photos? It's just a question of editing and splicing, isn't it?"

"Yes and no. But I'm not sure I'll have time for a while."

Again, it was as though Mr. Powers was responding less to what she actually said than to some concern or apprehension her words had triggered. When he began talking again, she had the impression of someone thinking out loud and unaware he was doing it.

"I suppose I could make it this Sunday if you feel that way," he said reluctantly. "It would be a little complicated. There's lunch with the Herberts, a few calls . . . If you're thinking of quitting I'd better talk to you first."

"I didn't say anything about quitting. I've temporarily run out of steam. If you could just hold off on sending me more things for a while . . ."

"Listen, we'll talk about it a week from Sunday, okay? I'm sure you'll do your best until then."

Elaine sat there for a moment after he hung up, then reached into the desk's bottom drawer for the menu she had saved from their lunch. She had put it away without showing it to her mother, telling herself it would be nice to look at some day, not daring to think she might see him again so soon. Without really knowing why, she took it out and propped it up on her desk where she could see it while she worked.

That night during dinner she went over their conversation again, worrying that she might have complained too much about John. But it had almost seemed as if Mr. Powers *expected* her to complain—as if he felt most comfortable in the coaxing-resisting-yielding pattern that had marked their relationship right from the start. What she had said about being overwhelmed certainly wasn't true. If anything, she welcomed extra work, the more time-consuming and absorbing the better. Days when she finished early, there was her new, growing self-pity waiting for her like a chronic pain, content to bide its time until she had sufficient leisure to suffer. She decided that this was the reason she felt the need to stop working on John for the time being—she was in danger of becoming jealous of him, of everything he had had while he was growing up. There were no newspaper clippings of her as a young girl, no formal portraits in gilded frames. Except for a few pictures, the only perfectly intact past thing from her childhood to have survived the fire was a "slam book" she had kept in school the year she was thirteen—a loose-leaf notebook filled with lists of favorite records and favorite teachers, autographs, doodles of coy-looking cocker spaniels and rabbits with floppy ears. Even then she had been turned toward the past, listing as her favorite singer Johnny Ray, her favorite book *Char-*

lotte's Web, which her father had read out loud to her before he left for Korea, her favorite boyfriend Timmy Schefler, who had kissed her by the swings in fifth grade. What wasn't nostalgia was fantasy. Her favorite occupation had been "ballet dancer," her favorite place, "Paris, France," her greatest ambition "To live in a big house in the country with old-fashioned furniture and palominos."

That was all there was. Report cards with her hard-earned A's, a treasured doll, toy rings from gum machines, all had been destroyed. After the fire she'd never bothered saving very much, not even from the two dreamlike affairs she'd had in Boston before moving home. There hadn't been much to save in the first place, certainly not enough to give her the kind of romantic past she dreamed about sometimes, a past documented with passionate little notes, foolish mementos and sentimental gifts. For two brief affairs, there were two lonely past things: a term paper with "See me" scrawled across the top; a red balloon with the words "Blessing of the Fleet 1967" stamped across one deflated, dusty side.

She wasn't sure why she still kept them. She didn't take them out very much any more, and when she did she often confused the memories she had of both men into one. Each had been a professor she had had a crush on long before he asked her out; each had recently lost a wife, the history professor to cancer, the art professor through divorce; each attracted her most when he was vague and remote and lost his magic as he became more definite and real. The affairs had been similiar, too. Each had included enough pain to make her reluctant ever to get involved with anyone else; and enough pleasure to make her forget about the bad parts sometimes and long to start over again with someone new. What the past things recalled was less some particular event than the warm, almost nostalgic feeling she had momentarily felt toward both men, the feeling that each could satisfy the emptiness she had been aware of all her life. Before she knew them, she would walk alone across the bridge in the Public Gardens, feeling beautiful and frustrated at the same time, possessed by the illusion that any second a strong, handsome man would detach himself from the crowd and take her in his arms. Somebody out there cherished her—she was certain of it—but try as she might, she couldn't find out who.

For a while, she had thought it was Peter. He first attracted her because of the passion he brought to his history lectures. He stood in front of the class completely lost in whatever it was he happened to be talking about, shaking his head in anger at something that had happened fourteen hundred years ago, slapping his hand against the blackboard so hard that the chalk flew off and dusted his clothes. The term paper with its little note had been the first sign that he noticed her. That afternoon in his office she had been surprised to find that despite his rages he was a very gentle man, and it wasn't long before she convinced herself that this was the balm her emptiness had needed all along: gentleness, someone to talk with her in a quiet voice, someone to hold her hand. He had coaxed her slowly out of her shyness, taking her to nearby museums at first, driving her into the country for lunches in old inns, finally, a week before the term ended, asking her up to his lakeside cottage in Maine.

That summer she had gone back home to be with her mother. By the time she returned in the autumn, he had moved to a larger campus in the Midwest, leaving her with a soft, wistful kind of sadness she had indulged herself in during the semester it took to find someone else, this time in the art department—a tall bone of a man whose masculine self-confidence contrasted with his Southern accent in a way that enchanted all the women in his class, not just Elaine. As Peter had convinced her that gentleness was what she longed for, Jason persuaded her that what she needed was someone to make every decision for her, to tell her what to feel, what to think and to say. And Jason had certainly filled this role to perfection. One night over cocktails he had admitted to her that his heroes had always been the great dictators and that as a boy he had collected pictures of Stalin the way other boys collected pictures of Joe DiMaggio.

The following morning they had driven to Gloucester to sketch the fishing boats. Bored, he insisted they go home early; enthralled, she urged that they stay. They argued; she remained behind when he drove off, taking a bus back to Boston later in the day, clutching the small red balloon he had bought for her that morning like a rebellious little girl determined not to cry.

A slam book. A few photos. A reminder of one affair's beginning, another affair's end. It wasn't much, but at least it was something. What scrapbooks her mother had were in even worse shape than the home movies. Whole pages had been torn out, captions were smudged and illegible, bindings eaten away by invisibly small paper worms that left a chalky white excrement up and down the margins. Sometimes, late in the afternoon when she had finished working on John for the day, she would take out these old scrapbooks. She had promised her mother she would at least try to repair them. One Christmas when they were looking through them, a page had fallen out, and her mother had burst into tears. Here was Elaine at the zoo by herself, Elaine at Coney Island by herself, her mother (changing places now, handing her the camera with a warning about holding it still) standing alone by the seals, her mother walking alone down the boardwalk in her fur even though it was May and people were staring. There were empty pages and blank photos, blank like the movies they used to try to take of the squirrels they fed in Central Park, which turned out to be frame after frame of tilting green grass with only an occasional grayish blur to show a squirrel was actually there.

The Powers's home movies, of course, turned out to be just the opposite: crisp, professional, filled with relatives and friends. As with the photographs, there was no problem in editing John away;

by the time she finished a reel, the workshop floor was covered with strips of discarded film, each frame of which contained another part of him. It was while she was sweeping them up, trying to decide where to put them, that the solution first occurred to her.

"Why not?" she thought, going over to the closet where she kept her mother's films. Hadn't she always wondered what would happen if she tried it? It would be an experiment more than anything. A way of keeping up her interest. She took a reel from a box labelled "Squirrels, 1953" and brought it over to the splicing machine with a strip she had already cut away from the Powers's film. There was really no problem once she began.

Leaning closer, squinting, she threaded the films through the viewfinder until both overlapped.

"Oh, look!" her mother said that Sunday, pointing toward the screen. "There he goes, Elaine!"

Her mother always spotted the squirrel first, up in the right-hand corner about an inch below the top of the screen. Elaine slowed the projector down before it disappeared.

"It's a lovely brown one, Elaine," she said, in the same squealy way she had said it thirty years before. Her mother considered herself an authority on New York squirrels.

"Yes, Mommy. I remember that one all right."

Elaine was watching very carefully now, curious to see what her mother's reaction would be.

"Can you see, Mommy?"

"Fine, my love."

"I'm not going too fast for you?"

"No. It's just right."

The squirrel hopped off into the living room drapes. There were a few frames with nothing except white, then a boy dressed in a baseball uniform appeared standing on a sloping lawn beneath a tall oak tree. There was an intent, expectant look on his face; he seemed to be waiting for the camera. Off to his right, looking very far away because of the differences in film quality, was a skinny little girl of about the same age, lobbing acorns at a much smaller tree. You couldn't see the squirrel any more. The splice made it seem that she was throwing a ball toward the waiting boy.

"Oh, look Mommy," Elaine said softly, not even sure she was still awake. "There's John."

Her mother raised her head from the cushion long enough to stare at him, then let it drop back sleepily against the pillow. She didn't seem surprised at seeing him there.

"Wasn't that nice, Mommy? Shall I run that part through again?"

"I don't think so, Elaine. Not tonight. They were awfully greedy squirrels that day."

Elaine had only done it on a whim, but that night when she was helping her mother into bed (pulling stocking down right leg, rolling stocking down over swollen left knee, unwrapping bandages off ankles, placing circulation pills near alarm clock, turning night light on, rubbing ointment over back), Mrs. Collier asked about him.

"My memory is going bad on me, love. Who was that nice little boy you were playing with in the park?"

"Why that was John, Mommy. Don't you remember John?"

Her eyes didn't focus, but she nodded her head.

"Oh, John," she said. "Of course."

"Shh now. Time to go to sleep."

A whim, Elaine thought, tucking her mother in, leaving the door open a crack so she could hear her if she got up, because it was silly letting the leftover threads and cuts from John's life go to waste in the trash—because she wanted in some way, in *any* way, to change the monotonous, empty past of those Sunday afternoons. It was her justification for accepting Mr. Powers's invitation—a change of scenery, a chance to escape her routine. He picked her up around one. ("There's egg salad in the refrigerator, Mrs. Peabody. She takes her nap once she's done. Under no circumstances allow her near the front door.") They visited the Whitney first, then walked toward the East River, enjoying the sunshine, Mr. Powers a bit ahead of her, his overcoat blowing open in the wind, Elaine a step or two behind, not feeling quite as awkward as she had the first time at the restaurant, enjoying herself in a way she hadn't for years. They had lunch in a bar on York Avenue. Mr. Powers told her about his business and asked her about her own background but said very little about John.

For Elaine, the afternoon ended too soon. She loved the crowds they passed on the street, the feeling of warmth in the March air, the sense that here anything was possible. The afternoon was like a scrapbook, reminding her of the days when she had lived by herself in Boston in a vivid, immediate way that neither Peter's term paper nor Jason's balloon could summon. She rode back to Queens in Mr. Powers's sports car feeling free and nostalgic at the same time, brushing the hair out of her eyes with the same gesture a person uses in turning a page.

"I want to thank you again," she said when he dropped her off. "Once again, I had a wonderful time."

"That's what I like to hear."

He reached over to take something off the back seat.

"Here are John's letters, from prep school through college. He used to have this girlfriend of sorts. These are some of the letters he wrote to her."

There were several dozen envelopes held together with a frayed rubber band. Elaine, thumbing through them, was surprised to find that at least half had never been opened. When she asked him about this, he shrugged.

"We read a few of them. There were so many, though. Carol finds it distressing. They're all pretty much the same: I miss you; I'm lonely. That kind of thing. It was a very one-sided relationship."

"On her side?"

"On his."

All this time he had been nervously rubbing his hand around the top of the steering wheel. Elaine knew that there was a point beyond which he found it difficult to talk about John. At lunch he had begun to tell her more about his death, only to end up groping for the name of the place where he was killed. Elaine felt sorry for him when he talked this way, but she was, if anything, even more attracted to him at these times than she was when he was being his usual, self-assured self. She had never pitied a man before, and it was only now that she realized what an appealing emotion it could be. Peter's gentleness, Jason's authority—neither had seemed as compelling as this.

"You found them too painful to read, didn't you?" Elaine said gently. "I can understand that. But this girl . . . you mean she never even opened them?"

"She ended up marrying a lawyer while John was overseas," Mr. Powers said. "Colin Tyndal. Does some work for my plant as a matter of fact. His parents are in our club. I suppose she was embarrassed at still getting the letters, so she used to bring them over to us just the way she got them. I don't think John ever found out before he . . . before he . . . John had peculiar ideas about women."

"Peculiar how?"

"Too demanding. Romantic with a capital R. He wanted them the All-American girl-next-door type to begin with, but he wanted more besides. A cheerleader with brains. Kathy was the cheerleader all right, but that's as deep as she went."

Elaine put the letters down. "There must be fifty here. What am I supposed to do with them all?"

"I thought you could keep some and send some back, the way you've been doing. If there are any painful parts, they could be cut out or rearranged so Carol wouldn't notice. I'll let her look through the ones you return, then gradually, when she's feeling better, I'll send you those, too. After that I don't care. Burn them, throw them out. Carol doesn't seem to talk about him quite as obsessively as she used to."

Something—his tone, his sudden mention of his wife—irritated Elaine. "You'll be sending me his shoes and socks next," she said, turning away from him.

"What's that supposed to mean?"

"Nothing. I've got to say good-by now."

She started unbuckling her seat belt. Mr. Powers reached over and took hold of her wrist to stop her.

"You're not angry at me, are you? I hope not, because I've just had a brilliant idea. There's an opera next month I'm dying to hear, but Carol doesn't particularly care for music. Shall I try for a couple of tickets for a Sunday matinee? It would be nice having someone to share it with. We could have dinner afterward."

"There's my mother," Elaine said automatically.

"Can't you get Mrs. Whatever to stay? I'd really like you to come."

"That's very nice, but I'm so busy right now. I have this man's stamp collection to straighten up, and there are still these old films coming in . . ."

He still had hold of her wrist. He squeezed it now—squeezed it hard like a teacher who has caught his pupil in a fib.

"No, that's not true," Elaine said, shaking her head. "I made that up. I could go if I wanted to. It's just . . . it's just not the kind of thing I'm used to any more, that's all."

"Which is why I want you to take your time and think it over. Call me when you decide."

"I really don't think I'll be able to."

"If I say please?"

Elaine laughed despite herself. "All right. I'll seriously consider it, but that's all I can promise."

"That's all I want. See you soon!"

Elaine waited until he turned the corner, then ran up the steps in a girlish way that made her want to giggle. She was fumbling in her purse for the keys when the door abruptly swung open.

"Your mother!" Mrs. Peabody shrieked, her face white, her whole body trembling. "Your mother, your mother, your mother!"

Mrs. Collier always liked taking a walk after her nap. She wanted to ask Mrs. Peabody if she would like to go, too, but Mrs. Peabody was sound asleep on the living-room couch.

"Mrs. Peabody?" she whispered. "If you like, I thought we could go for a nice little stroll. It's such a glorious day out, Mrs. Peabody. Mrs. Peabody?"

Mrs. Peabody snored.

"I thought we could visit Mildred in the sanatorium, then take the trolley to New York and see Uncle Fred. He has a carting business, Mrs. Peabody. Sometimes he lets me feed the ponies."

"That's nice," Mrs. Peabody mumbled, her mouth drooping open. Mrs. Collier went over to close it for her, but the moment she touched her cheek it snapped shut by itself.

Perhaps, on second thought, it would be better to go alone. Mrs. Collier returned to her bedroom for a sweater in case it got cold and went into Elaine's room for the carfare that was always scattered across the top of her dresser.

"Oh dear!"

There were only three nickels this time. It wasn't nearly enough. She would have to change trolleys at least twice, and she wanted to buy sugar for the ponies as well. She rummaged through the dresser until she found a small calfskin purse hidden away in the bottom drawer underneath some panties. She put it in her pocketbook, left a note on Elaine's pillow telling her where she would be, then went back to the living room to see if Mrs. Peabody had changed her mind.

"I'm off, Mrs. P."

Mrs. Peabody looked cold. She held her arms tucked tight

against her chest like a squirrel hugging acorns. Mrs. Collier covered her up with a shawl off the love seat, then quietly, with a last look behind her, started tiptoeing down the stairs toward the forbidden front door.

The sun stung her eyes at first. She stood on the front stoop deliberately facing it, blinking her eyelids until she got used to its brightness. Adie had taught her that trick at Rockaway Beach. Adie was good about those things.

"There are just two dangers a girl must learn to watch for, Viola," she would say over tea. "Saucy firemen who try to steal a kiss and dishonest butchers who put their thumbs on the scale when you're not looking."

She was certainly right about the sun. Gradually, Mrs. Collier found she could face it without squinting. She reached into her pocketbook to make sure of the carfare, wrapped the sweater around her neck like a scarf and started across the middle of the street toward Woodhaven Avenue.

"Hey, watch it, lady! You wanna get killed?"

It was such a beautiful day out; it was a shame Mrs. Peabody had decided not to come. There were robins hopping along the curb, pecking at buns, the doves were making a lovely cooing sound up on the roofs, and Mrs. Collier just knew it wouldn't be long before she spotted her first squirrel.

"Good morning, Mrs. Davidson. How are you today?"

"*Por favor?*"

There were so many people out strolling she knew—she kept nodding and saying hello all the way to the corner. Once there she had to make a decision: visit Mildred first, or go see Uncle Fred and stop at the sanatorium on the way home. If she waited too long to see Fred, the horses might already have eaten. If, on the other hand, she went to New York first, visiting hours might be over by the time she got back.

"I'd like to see Mildred Sayers, please," she said to the man at the gate.

"Who?"

"Mildred Sayers, please. She has a moist spot on her right lung."

"I don't know what you're talking about, lady," the man snorted. He had a rake with him. He was pulling leaves off the end like someone cleaning a comb.

"Room Eight B. Although I would prefer to visit her in the solarium if you don't mind."

"And I'm Santa Claus."

He started raking the leaves as if he were mad at them. Mrs. Collier was becoming a bit irritated herself.

"Mildred Sayers has been in this sanatorium for seven years come Easter. She's a Methodist. I always visit her on Sundays. Obviously you must be new here."

"Lady, this is *not* a sanatorium. Not any more leastwise. This place has been boarded up ever since I can remember, and me and the wife have lived in this neighborhood since before the war. And don't go asking me what they intend to do with it either. I don't know nothing, I don't want to know nothing. Bunch of spooks in there if you ask me. All these goddamn Puerto Rican kids shooting their arms full of God knows what. You think the cops care? As far as I'm concerned, the place could burn down tomorrow, good riddance."

Mrs. Collier could see she was getting nowhere. "In that case I'll speak with Doctor Thomas, please."

"Listen, Grandma, you're very sweet and all, but let me clue you in on something for your own good. Beat it! Got that? Scram on out of here! There's nothing left here any more but ghosts. Ghosts, potheads, leaves, that's it."

Maybe it would be better to visit Uncle Fred first after all. She thanked the gatekeeper for his help in what she hoped was a suitably withering tone, recrossed Woodhaven and started toward Jamaica Avenue to catch the trolley. It was so warm and sunny out she decided she didn't need the sweater after all. She left it carefully folded on a bench near the Masonic Hall where it would be safe until she came back. At the same time it occurred to her that it might be nice to surprise Elaine by stopping at O'Reilly's to buy some meat for dinner.

"Good morning, Miss O'Reilly. Two pounds of your best chuck if you please."

"My name is Sheldon, lady. Mrs. Sheldon. There is nobody here that other name. But you want hamburger, this is the spot."

She was apparently suffering from a cold. Her eyes were watering and she kept bending down to wipe her nose off on her apron.

"*Two* pounds," Mrs. Collier said severely, pressing right up against the meat counter so she could watch. It wasn't a good idea getting too friendly with shopkeepers. You couldn't afford to take your eyes off them for a second.

The lady slapped some meat on the scale, wiped her nose off, then dribbled on a scrap or two more.

"I said *two* pounds, Miss O'Reilly. No use trying to cheat me. I'm sure I don't have to remind you how long my family's been buying here. We literally paid for your brother's passage."

Shrugging, the lady rubbed the palm of her hand along the cutting board until she had a dab the size of a meatball, then, after holding it up for Mrs. Collier's approval, slapped it down on top of the scale with the rest. It brought the pointer a shade past two. Mrs. Collier smiled a triumphant little smile and reached into her pocketbook.

"How much will that be, Miss O'Reilly?"

"For you, lady? For you, we make it $3.93."

Mrs. Collier felt much better once the meat was safely wrapped and she was outside again. People were coming back from the Congregational church now and she was kept busy saying hello to the ones she knew.

"Hello, Mrs. Cossy. Hello, Miss Rogers. Hello, Larry, hello, Mike. Gorgeous hat, Lilly. Why hello there, Joe!"

By the corner of Jamaica Avenue she had given up saying hello to anyone. She walked along the sidewalk with the meat tucked securely in the crook of her right arm, her eyes fixed safely on the pavement, hoping any of her friends who saw her would realize she was much too rushed to stop. But even without having to say hello, things started going wrong. She waited on the corner for half an hour without a single trolley stopping, even though she signaled for them with her hat. It was maddening. It was worse than maddening, it was inexcusable. She was trying to summon up the nerve to ask a stranger what the delay might be when with a great surge of relief she spotted a clean-shaven young policeman standing next to a nearby hot-dog wagon drinking pop.

"Excuse me, officer," she said. "I wonder if you can help me. I'm waiting here for the Brooklyn trolley, but it doesn't seem to come."

The young man put down the bottle and looked at her with interest.

"Wow," he said at last, shaking his head. "You're really going to have to wait a long time, ma'am."

This information irritated her no end.

"I don't see why, officer. They never had trouble on this line."

"Are you for real, ma'am? No offense or anything, but I wondered. You just escape?"

"If I don't get to Fred's by twelve then there's no use going, is there, officer?"

The young man looked around to see if anyone was watching, then took her by the elbow and walked her up the street away from the crowd.

"You think I'm a cop, right? Forget it. I ain't no cop. I'm a messenger. Three bucks an hour plus this lousy hat. My brother Chris got me the job, I think it sucks."

Adie's husband Tom was a policeman. Mrs. Collier wondered if he would know him. She was on the point of asking him when he broke in with a question of his own.

"You want to guess how old I am, ma'am? Nineteen. I don't

look that old, do I? It's on account of this peach fuzz on my bottom lip here. See? I don't shave yet, ma'am. Don't you think that's kind of weird for a guy my age? You don't think maybe I'm stunted, do you?"

"Perhaps if I were to wait on the opposite corner?"

"No, ma'am, I wouldn't do that if I were you. A lot of those teenage gangs hang out over there. You never know what they're going to do if you come too close."

"All I want is to find the trolley, officer."

"You know, that's really interesting. All that history I mean. I bet you remember Jamaica the way it looked back in the olden days, right? That kills me. I mean that it could ever have looked different than this. I'm really into history, ma'am. You wouldn't think that to look at me, would you?"

"I'd take a cab, but they're so dear these days. I'm afraid Elaine didn't leave me much money."

"Where'd you say you were going, ma'am? Brooklyn? I've been there once. Nothing special if you know what I mean. A lot like Queens. But you want to go? I mean, you want, we could take the subway. I'll tell you something straight out, ma'am. You're a really nice lady. I don't meet many nice ladies being a messenger. I go to these offices with these knockout secretaries sitting there with their skirts hitched up, and they look through me like I'm glass."

Mrs. Collier shifted the meat to her left arm.

"I don't particularly like subways," she said.

"Oh, it's okay," the young man said. "I'm not one of those rapists or anything. I wouldn't do that to a nice lady, I promise. Anyway, I'm not going to be a lousy messenger for long. I've got plans, ma'am. I'm going to get a job in one of those computer outfits. I'm going to learn all about it at home and get one of those jobs you see in the paper and make it big. I'll be walking down Jamaica Avenue this time next year with ten knockout secretaries drooling all over me."

"They're noisy and they smell."

"Mister Big Shot, that's me. See my Cadillac back there? I'm going to have a red one, ma'am. I'm going to get a big house in the country and drive all around Jamaica like nobody can stop me."

"Elaine doesn't like me talking to strangers."

"Hello, foxy! No, I can't make it tonight, baby. I've got some other knockout chick coming over. Yeah, I'm flying to Spain next week, wanna come? I'm making it big in computers, walking down this street like I'm king . . . What did you say, ma'am?"

"Elaine doesn't like me talking to strangers."

"But I'm a policeman, ma'am. Didn't you say so before?"

He stopped her outside a bakery and said something in a voice that was less shrill than before but more urging.

"I think it's time we went down to the subway, ma'am. We could get to Brooklyn that way, no problem."

"I don't particularly care for subways."

"They're okay once you get to know them. Hey, listen! I'll take care of you. I told you that, right? Here, we'll just walk down the stairs here . . ."

"I don't want to!" Mrs. Collier whispered, holding back.

"Move!"

Mrs. Collier started to cry.

"Hey, listen, ma'am. I'm sorry. I didn't mean to scare you like that. You okay? Here, just follow me, we'll go down to Fred's or whatever his name is this way."

Mrs. Collier followed him reluctantly down the stairs to the station. It was cold and terribly damp inside. She remembered her sweater and started shivering.

"You cold, ma'am? If you are, I could warm you up. Here, why don't you stand over there against the wall this way. No, just a little bit farther down here where it's nice and dark and quiet."

"Are you sure this is the Brooklyn platform?"

The young man didn't seem to hear her. He was fussing with her blouse as if he had spotted a loose thread on it and was trying to pull it off. At the same time he seemed out of breath. He was panting, his hat had fallen off. And it was at this moment that Mrs. Collier suddenly began to realize that he wasn't a policeman after all.

"Boy, you're really a nice lady, you know that, ma'am? You're really built for an old lady. I really like you, ma'am. I want to kiss you and feel you and . . ."

He was a fireman!

Mrs. Collier screamed.

The young man ran up the stairway. Mrs. Collier held onto a gum machine for support, listening to her scream chase after him down the tunnel. The sound didn't diminish the way most echoes did. It repeated itself off the nearby walls at the level at which she had emitted it, then seemed, as it moved out of the il-luminated part of the station, to pick up volume and speed, becoming louder and louder before suddenly reversing directions and coming back to her like a boomerang, so loud she had to put her fingers in her ears. Just when it became loudest, just when she felt ready to faint, a refreshing stream of cool air blew against her cheek—she opened her eyes. There snapping open in front of her were the in-gathering doors of the BMT local, Brooklyn bound.

She found a seat in the corner where she wouldn't have to look at anyone. To make sure, she twisted sideways in her seat until the little rat-faced man sitting across the aisle was out of sight. To make doubly sure, she closed her eyes.

"Hey, lady? You asleep?"

There was a trick Adie had taught her to pass the time: think of all the nice occasions you had experienced since your last birthday, try to remember who else had been involved. Some-times she varied this by thinking of Thanksgiving, trying to count the relatives sitting around Fred's huge table. Other times she would try to remember who got what for Christmas, or what she'd had to eat every meal for the past five days. Breakfast was easy because she always had the same thing every morning, sausages and buns. Yesterday dinner was easy, too, and sometimes she could even remember yesterday lunch. But no matter how hard she tried, no matter how many combinations of meats and vegetables she came up with, she could never remember day-before-yesterday dinner, let alone day-before-yesterday lunch.

Mrs. Collier felt someone tugging at her wrist.

"Go away," she mumbled.

What she liked best was thinking about all the boys she had gone out with that year. She started with Dick Schaefer and worked her way past him to Benny Dolan . . .

"One," she said, counting off the stops.

Past Benny Dolan to Jacob Theosen, the Swedish carpenter who tried to get her to take a steambath, past him to Paul Cooper, past Paul to Frank Collier . . .

"Two!"

But no matter how many times she tried it, she never got past Frank. When she first met him he had been working in a Bible warehouse near where her Uncle Alan lived, stacking Bibles. They hadn't hit it off at first. He was three years younger than she was for one thing. She thought he was far too brash and sure of himself to be much good.

"Three!"

It had not been until their second date—the time in March he had led her inside a bar for the first time in her life—that she had thought she might like him after all. It had been very dark and cool there. Someone was playing Benny Goodman on the jukebox, and Frank had wanted to dance. The foam off their beers left mustaches across their lips, and they giggled when they caught each other's eyes in the mirror behind the bar.

"Four!"

She swayed back and forth with the motion of the car, counting off the stations until it was time to get out, concentrating on the image of Frank in his new uniform, Frank coming shyly up the steps to propose. People were already starting to call her an old maid behind her back by then. She had worried about his aimless drifting from job to job, but she had loved him too much to say no.

"Five! Oh dear!"

Her pocketbook was gone. It wasn't on her lap—it wasn't on the seat. She got down on her hands and knees to look underneath the seat, but it wasn't there either. Before she had a chance to search any farther the crowd wedged her out through the door, out past the turnstiles, upstairs to the street.

Now that she'd lost the pocketbook there was no convenient place for her hands. She sat propped against a hydrant near the corner of Fulton trying to catch her breath, rubbing the back of her thumb over the spot on her cheek where the fireman had kissed her. If she had still had the sweater she could have carried it under her right arm and pretended the pocketbook was tucked away under that. As it was she had nothing except the meat. She turned it wrapper side out and dangled it under her arm, hoping people would think it was a handbag.

"Good afternoon! I'm collecting for public television's fund-raising campaign. As you're probably aware, our motto this year is 'Watching without pledging is equivalent to theft.' "

"I'm voting for Roosevelt, thank you," Mrs. Collier said, walking right around her.

Blood was oozing out of the bag. It left a little trail of bright red specks on the sidewalk that reminded her of Mildred when she coughed. If she had been more polite to the girl she could have asked for a Willkie flyer to cover her head with. The sun had gone out while she was underground. There were clouds blowing in from the lower harbor, and they threatened rain.

"Good afternoon! I'm collecting for Columbia House drug rehabilitation center. I wonder if you would care to make a small contribution. Let's get the pushers off the street!"

"My husband is in the army," Mrs. Collier said, brushing his arm away. "I think that's contribution enough, don't you?"

She was feeling too tired to buy any bonds. Tired and funny in the stomach and vaguely dizzy. If she had had any nickels left, she would have gone into the nearest automat for coffee. As it was, there wouldn't be a chance to get anything before Fred's. He always kept a slice of raisin cake from lunch for her and there was sure to be hot cider or tea. The only problem was it was taking so long to get there. For some reason, it seemed that the closer she got to the bridge, the farther away Fred's stable became.

"Vote for Truman!" she chanted, brushing past their flyers. "Vote for Truman!"

She had never known Fulton Street to be so crowded. She forced her way along the outside of the sidewalk wishing she had stayed home. Sometimes when it was crowded like this she began having dreams, terrible dreams that kept her awake. Dreams about the future, dreams where everything and everyone she had known since she was a girl were blotted out by swarms of ugly, hard-looking midgets who spoke a different language too rapidly for her to understand. She would dream she was walking along like this on a beautiful Sunday afternoon without running into a single person she knew—dream of a huge cloud of noxious, cloying smoke descending over the skyline across the river, spoiling the view. Smoke so black and thick it made her choke, even that far away.

"Vote for Truman," she mumbled.

Her eyes watered from the cloud. Her ears ached from the midgets' shrill voices. Her stomach felt queasy.

"Vote for Truman," she whispered, barely able to move. "Vote for Truman."

She reached the bridge just in time. There was hardly anyone on it now that the sun had gone in; she looked up and down its entire length, but fortunately the midgets were all gone. She felt much better now. Looking at the soft, effortless way the bridge arched itself across the river made her feel lighthearted herself, as though its lacelike cables, its gentle, yearning curve were sunny rays emitted from her own sense of well-being.

She took a deep, satisfied breath and started across, humming to herself, lifting her feet up in march step. "Oh, I wish I were in the land of cotton, old times there are not forgotten, look away, look away, look . . ."

She had another dizzy spell halfway across, this one much worse than before. She leaned against the railing to keep from fainting, the wind blowing her hair over her eyes until she couldn't see. She turned away, but it was no use. The cloud came back again, even more acrid and choking. It was the color of iodine, not black—a reddish-yellow that settled over her like a gas and found its way down the openings in her clothes until she started shivering.

Everyone she knew would die some day. All the boys she had gone out with, all her aunts and uncles and cousins, all the ponies in Fred's barn. They would all die, and she would be left alone among strangers in a strange world she didn't understand. The thought of this made her feel very sad. She stood there listening to the moaning sound the wind made between the cables and started to cry.

It was too far to walk to New York. It was too far to walk back to Brooklyn. No matter which way she turned she kept bumping into it, the red-yellow haze, wrapping itself around her like a plastic bag, smothering, refusing to go away no matter how madly she swung her arms about, no matter how often she cried for help.

"Frank! Frank!"

And it was just at the worst moment that she spotted him swimming far below in the chocolate brown of the white-capped river. He was swimming backstroke under the bridge. For a moment the bridge hid him, and she held her breath until he reappeared on the uptown side, paddling stubbornly as ever toward Hell's Gate.

"Frank!"

He didn't see her. He was swimming very easily and powerfully toward shore and was too busy looking backward to look up and see her on the bridge.

"Wait for me, Frank!"

She would surprise him. She would jump in and land with a splash beside him, and they could swim toward shore together, just the two of them, the same way they coasted in with the waves at Rockaway Beach during the summer. She would swim backstroke while he turned on his stomach beside her and tickled her toes like a crab.

"Wait! I'm coming! I'm coming, Frank!"

She would jump in, and they would swim together up the river past Hell's Gate, kissing the salt off each other's lips, treading water, floating up past the docks with the tide, under all the other bridges, Frank calling out their names like a trolley conductor as they drifted beneath, drifted past pennant-strung ferries loaded with children, past small pilot boats whose skippers saluted them with their whistles as they chugged by, past fishermen, past freighters whose wash tumbled them gently over like seals, the sun setting on the breaking crests . . . drifting, drifting . . . until finally they escaped time's river completely and emerged on an unfamiliar yet welcome shore, hand in hand, into a garden, into the garden there to dry among the shade of trees in fragrant blossom.

Joyfully, with the grand gesture someone would use in christening a proud ship, Mrs. Collier climbed on top of the railing and threw the meat over the side of the bridge.

Major Haig-Brown died in April. He collapsed while visiting a neighbor at the hospital, falling backward, ramrod-straight, arms flung out at either side, as though hit by a bullet fired years before. The doctors had him carried to the next room, but it was a massive stroke, and he wasn't given long to live.

It couldn't have come at a worse time for Elaine. Only a week had gone by since her mother's day of freedom; by the time the police car brought her home—Mrs. Collier nodding, smiling, waving to either side like a queen being driven to her coronation—Elaine was nearly overwhelmed by worry, and she was was still feeling emotionally drained when she received the bad news about the major in a phone call from a sobbing Olga. At first Elaine was afraid to leave her mother alone again so soon, but the expedition to Brooklyn seemed to have assuaged something in her, and she acted more docile now, content with her imaginary journeys back and forth through the halls. Elaine decided to risk a short visit to the major during her mother's nap the afternoon after he collapsed.

There had been a freak storm the night before and the daffodils in the hospital garden were covered with fresh snow. Elaine picked one for him, but once indoors the flower immediately drooped. On her way to the elevator she found a trash basket and dropped it in.

The major was on the third floor in a room usually reserved for women in labor. He was lying unconscious near the window, tubes strapped to either arm, an oxygen mask taped awkwardly across his mouth. When Elaine reached down to straighten it, he gave a convulsive jerk with his arm and knocked her hand away, ripping out three of the tubes. Elaine, on the verge of tears, went to the corridor to find a nurse.

"Oh, now look what you've done!" the nurse said when she came in. "He's always up to his tricks, this one. A body can't get any rest nursing him."

"Do you think he's in much pain?" Elaine asked.

"Doesn't feel a thing, miss. Sometimes they can still hear, though. That's the last thing goes after a stroke. Their hearing, I mean. You come around here like this and yell in his ear. Maybe he'll catch a word or two."

"I don't think so, thank you," Elaine said, trying desperately to think of some excuse. "Uh, we're not related."

"That's okay. I'll make space for you."

Elaine had no choice. She went over to the bed and leaned down to his ear the way the nurse demonstrated.

"Major?"

"Oh, you'll have to do it louder than that."

"Major! It's me, Major. Elaine Collier!"

What was she supposed to watch for? Some convulsive jerk of acknowledgment from the region of the head? Some flutter of recognition in the eyelids? It was stupid. He was dead already. Elaine felt bitter that she should be forced to go through the motions over a dead man she had once loved, pretend with the nurse that he wasn't feeling anything except a mild curiosity as to voices, that he suffered no pain. Of course he suffered. His chest shook from the effort of breathing. His exhalations made a leaking sound halfway between a hiss and a scream. His entire body twitched in violent spasms that left him twisted sideways across the bed.

"He's resting comfortably," the nurse said, fluffing up his pillow.

And when Elaine finally left, after she had said good-by to him with a slight pressure of her middle three fingers against the pulse of his left wrist, his chest was still rising and falling with the same throbbing passion, as if nothing, no war, no fear, no regret, no sickness could ever quench the strong courageous instinct of that ever-beating heart.

The funeral was scheduled for Sunday. Elaine was invited over the phone in the course of a strange conversation with a woman she didn't know.

"Hello? Is this Elaine Collier? C, O, L, I, E, R?"

"Double L. Yes, it is."

"Your name is on my list. His list."

"Whose list?"

"Toward the top. As a matter of fact, the *very* top. His list, not mine. I don't keep lists. We found it in his phone book along with his laundry bills. I normally live in London."

"Who is this please?"

Elaine could hear her yelling at someone in the background. There was the sound of grunting, then a tremendous crash, as though a box of china had just been dropped.

"Hello?"

"The service is this Sunday. Two o'clock at Barrett's Funeral Home on Hillside Avenue. Do you know where that is?"

"Of course."

"Pardon?"

Elaine suddenly realized that the woman herself didn't know. She gave her directions, repeating them while whoever else was there with her wrote them down.

"Take a right at Woodhaven, then left on . . . Are you getting all this, Todd?"

After she hung up, Elaine went downstairs to the cabinet in her workshop where she kept the major's Somme flower. She had made only a half-hearted effort with it so far. Once the spring came, she had brought it upstairs to the sunlight and tried various plant foods and fertilizers, all to no visible effect.

She was feeling guilty about it. Guilty and angry at the same time. Having it there was too much of a burden for her, it had been inconsiderate of the major to give it to her in the first place. Now, with his death, it seemed as if he had deliberately plotted to saddle her with it all along.

It occurred to her that she had three options: to keep it locked away in the cabinet until years went by and she forgot what it was; to take it to the funeral home and give it to some member of the major's family; to place it in the coffin with the major's body and have it buried with him.

She couldn't stand the thought of the first. There were too many past things cluttering up her workshop as it was. Giving it back to the family would mean lengthy explanations she wasn't sure she would be in the mood for. Putting it in the coffin was melodramatic and probably just as hard. In the end, after considering simply throwing it away, she decided to bring it with her to the funeral and make the decision there.

When she called Mr. Powers to tell him she wouldn't be able to go to the opera, Mrs. Powers answered the phone.

"Just the person I wanted to speak to," she said in a way that Elaine thought sounded ominous. "In fact, I was just about to call you myself."

"About John's things?" Elaine asked cautiously.

"About John's things."

Elaine took a deep breath. "Are they all right?" she asked.

"They're splendid! But what I wanted to call you about was memory."

"Memory?"

"Yes, memory. It's funny, memory."

"Funny?"

"It does funny things. Here I remembered all these debating trophies John had, when of course there was only that one you polished up and sent back. Isn't that odd?"

"Memory can play strange tricks," Elaine said, in the same

tone of voice she used in humoring her mother. "By the way, does Mr. Powers happen to be home? There are some things I need his advice on. Business things," she added quickly.

"Just a minute and I'll get him."

Mrs. Powers didn't seem surprised at her asking for him. Elaine wondered about this. Had Mr. Powers said something to his wife about seeing her? Was she the latest flirtation in a long line? A potential recruit to a harem he no longer bothered to hide from his wife? When he came on the phone, he took the news of not seeing her so nonchalantly that she wondered whether he had been planning to break the date himself. It annoyed her that she should be feeling angry at this. "I haven't had a chance to work on your son lately," she said before hanging up. "I'm afraid I'm going to have to give him up fairly soon."

The funeral home was crowded with mourners by the time she got there. At first she assumed they were there for somebody else's funeral, and it wasn't until she managed to push her way from the coat room to the lobby that she discovered the major's was the only one scheduled for the afternoon.

"Welcome," the funeral director said, handing her a program. "Family or friend?"

"Friend."

"Friends in Chapel C, please. Service starts in fifteen minutes."

Elaine found a chair near the back. She could just see the top of the casket. It was closed—"Thank God," she thought—and covered with huge floral pieces that made the Somme flower tucked away in her pocketbook seem small and very humble.

"Nice turnout, eh?" the man sitting next to her said. He reeked of after-shave lotion, and Elaine had been trying to avoid looking in his direction.

"Very nice."

"You in the business?"

"No."

"What business you in?"

"I fly. Excuse me."

She found a seat in the corner. She had imagined there would be only four or five people there, had even pictured a pathetic little scene where no one turned up at all except herself. As it was, there must have been well over a hundred people inside the small chapel, with more coming in all the time. There was much fervent hand-shaking, a great many half-kissed cheeks—it made it seem more like a wedding reception than a funeral. Judging by the fragments of conversation she was able to overhear, most of the people were colleagues from the days when the major had worked in Manhattan.

It didn't take her long to decide she didn't belong there. For whatever reason, it was obvious that the major had deliberately concealed one side of his life from her. Or was it only her own sentimentality that had pictured him as lonely and forgotten? She wasn't sure, and the uncertainty about her own motives bothered her even more than the ostentatious suavity and easy regret of the other mourners. If nothing else, she told herself, he had revealed to her a portion of his past that he had apparently not seen fit to share with most people. There was no mention in the lengthy obituary printed inside the program of his ever having been in a war, no precious miniature of Catherine reproduced on its covers. It was as if the major, having relived his memories through Elaine and tried on their suffering again, had decided to die a civilian after all.

The late-arriving guests were just taking their seats when Elaine spotted Olga standing on tiptoes by the door, trying to see.

"Excuse me," she said, pushing past the knees in her aisle. "Excuse me, please . . . Olga!"

Olga waved. Everyone turned around to see what the commotion was. One of the funeral directors put his finger to his lips and shook his head severely back and forth. Elaine pointed to the door that led to the lobby, and Olga understood her at once. They managed to escape together a second before the service began.

"So!"

"How are you, Olga?"

"Crushed, that's how. I expected a nice quiet service, maybe some crying, maybe a sermon or two. Not Times Square. Where do they all come from?"

"I was just about to ask you the same question."

"That fancy lady up front I know. The man next to her I know. They've been tearing things apart upstairs all week like two Cossacks. But the rest? You know something, Elaine? I think the general's been holding out on us."

"Do you think we ought to stay?"

Olga shrugged. "Me, I already said good-by. The general was a nice man. A real English gentleman. I've had lots of tenants upstairs over the years, but he was the only real one. You know what I mean, Elaine, when I say real? The general was real. All those rest were phonies. I don't even remember what they looked like."

"I think I know, Olga. Shall we splurge and take a cab home?"

"Of course. Only let's keep an eye on the meter."

It wasn't far, but Olga acted like someone who had never ridden in a cab before, sitting very erect, legs straight out to brace herself, arms held tight against her side to act as bumpers when they went around curves.

"That was a *good* cab ride," she unexpectedly told the driver when he pulled up in front of her house. "Now you come in, Elaine, and say hello to Katya."

"I'd love to Olga, but my mother's alone today, and you know what that means."

"Phooey! She's in such a hurry you can't spare ten minutes? I know the general is gone now and you'll probably never come visit me any more . . ."

"You know that's not true, Olga. We'll set a date for dinner sometime next week."

"In the meantime you come in."

Elaine paid the cab driver. Olga unfastened the double locks on the door and led the way through the dim, dusty hall into the kitchen. Elaine blinked when Olga turned the lights on; Katya came up and rubbed her legs while Olga fixed coffee. It seemed strange being there without the major upstairs.

"Cream or sugar? With you I forget."

"Cream please. Olga, have I ever told you how much I admire your plants? You have a real talent."

"You like them?"

"They're beautiful."

Olga blushed. "See this one over here?" She pulled a small clay pot out from behind the African violets. "Two weeks ago it was dead. Mrs. Jacobi next door brought it over from her garden. It was nothing, just a dried-up piece of cabbage. But I took care of it, I watered it my special way, and now look—Miss America!"

Elaine saw her chance. "Olga, I know a plant that needs a good home. Will you rescue it, too?"

Olga shook her head and smiled. "I make no promises, but who knows? Sometimes miracles happen if you wish hard enough. But never mind the compliments, Miss Businessman. Here. Hold out your hand, close your eyes. What do you think about this?"

Olga had been holding something behind her back all the while they had been talking. She handed it to her now. It was a square piece of heavy cloth the size of a matchbook. At first Elaine assumed it was a swatch off a gray overcoat Olga wanted mended. It wasn't until Olga led her into the living room where the light was better that she realized she was mistaken. It wasn't gray, it was an indescribable brownish white flecked with black, and it felt like coarse burlap.

"Did you have a favorite party dress when you were small?" Olga asked abruptly. "One that was so special you always worried it might rip or get dirty?"

"Yes," Elaine lied.

"I did, too, but not the kind you would think about. There was a woman in our village who had danced in Vienna. Inge Lengyel. Poor Inge, we called her. She lived all alone with a little Pekingese dog. She had arthritis in her knees, and she used to sit all day with a shawl pulled over them to keep them warm. But she had a treasure she would show to girls she liked. It was the ballet dress she had worn in Vienna. It was all she had left, but you could tell when she pressed it against her body that it brought it all back to her. Vienna. Dancing. The years when her legs had been able to take her leaping across the stage. Inge's memory dress, we used to call it."

"You didn't take ballet lessons from her, Olga, did you? For some reason I just can't picture you in a tutu."

It was a clumsy thing to say, but Olga wasn't listening any more. She sat down on the dark end of the couch and lit a cigarette, something Elaine had never seen her do before. Her voice, once she began, was different, too. It was deeper, more earnest. Listening to its steady drone hypnotized Elaine. After five minutes she couldn't have summoned up the power to stop her even if she had wanted to. She was swept along with her, nodding little punctuation marks of sympathy and assent in the proper spots.

"It seems so long ago it's another person. This foolish little girl I used to be running around the village without a thought in her head. This little girl who used to lie there on the sofa resting after school, dreaming of new dresses and dances and boys. There was a special one, too. I won't tell you his name. He was very shy, but one day he finally got up the nerve to give this foolish girl a picture he had painted. It was of a cow. I don't remember much about it except for that. But the little girl was looking at it, thinking what an extraordinary cow it was, when the Germans came for her family. Boom, boom, boom on the door, just like that. My father. My mother. My sister. We were in the middle of supper, and my father asked them if we could finish first."

Olga shook her head. " 'We're not Jews,' my father said. He kept saying it over and over. But it didn't matter. We were on their list. My father was mayor. He had Jewish friends . . . We were on their list. The young man who led them even showed my father. We were on the top. I think my father was secretly pleased with that because after a while he stopped whispering."

Katya was rubbing herself along the heel of Olga's shoe, asking to be picked up. Olga put her on her lap, patting her head in between cigarette puffs.

"Did I ever tell you how I found her?"

"No, Olga." Elaine was confused at the sudden switch in mood.

"Last year I was walking around the block like I do in the afternoon when I saw a boy beating her with a stick. Beating her! She was tied to a tree so she couldn't run away. 'Stop that!' I yelled. The boy was red in the face. 'It's my cat, and I'll hit her when I feel like it,' he said. He was a bully, the same you saw in the camps. He even had a swastika sewn on his jacket from this gang he belonged to. I threatened to call for the police, and he ran away. When I reached down to pick her up, she pulled back like I was going to hit her, too. I talked to her very quiet, and finally she let me pick her up. I didn't even go home with her. I went right straight to the veterinarian's."

Katya made a purring sound and buried herself beneath Olga's arms.

"I felt so bad for her. So sorry. And you know why? Because that was me at the end of the war. Scared. Afraid of shadows. Homeless. Not a single picture of my family to remind me of them, not anything from the little girl I used to be. There were these Frenchmen in camp with us. They said they would take me home with them if there was no one else. I lived in Paris for five years teaching Polish. You didn't know that about your old friend, did you? The little girl who wanted to be glamorous, teaching

Polish. But they saved me, Elaine. They saved me the same way I saved Katya."

"She's a beautiful cat," Elaine said, feeling idiotically trite. But Olga didn't seem to hear. She stubbed out the end of her cigarette on the ashtray and took a deep, shivering breath, like someone about to plunge into an ice-choked pool.

"When we got to camp that first time, they took our clothes away and gave us pajamas. 'How ugly!' everyone thought. But this foolish little girl thanked the soldier who threw them at her like they were a gown made of silk. She put them on thinking, 'How lovely I must look in my new dress!' All around her people were looking away from each other, feeling ashamed they should be forced to wear such a thing. Before they took him to another camp, my father used to tease me about it. 'Olga and her ball gown,' he would say. And you know what? To this little girl, it *was* a ball gown. She decided that first day that whatever happened she wouldn't let them become ugly prison pajamas. They must always be her link to the happy years. They must be her secret place nothing they could do would ever touch."

A car door slammed outside. For a moment Elaine was afraid it was the major's relatives coming back for his furniture, but after a moment the engine started up again, and the car moved away.

"She fussed over it like the vainest girl you can think of. Any rip, any little tear, she was desperate. She borrowed thread from the women in the hut to mend it. In summer when they let us have water, she would wash it and sit there naked on the floor waiting for it to dry, pressing out wrinkles with her hand. Two years she did that. Two years! No matter where they took her. These others would say to themselves, 'Well, if I am to live here I must do such and such or so and so.' They would steal. They would inform. But for this little girl, it was her dress. While all around people were dying, she worried about keeping her dress mended. Can you understand that? Living and keeping her dress pretty were the same things after a while. Even when the war was over. The others couldn't wait to be rid of their uniforms. The English brought a big truck with clothes they took from German families in town. 'Help yourselves,' they said. This little girl was so weak her friends had to find a dress for her. A dress and shoes. She put them on, but she refused to give up her uniform. She carried it rolled up under her arm all the way to France. Times when she was feeling lonely she would take it out from the drawer and mend it just like she was still in camp. She would sit sewing, thinking about mother and father and sister, and all the loneliness would go away."

It was dark out now. The one lamp still on was hardly enough to light up Olga's face. Somewhere deep inside the house the furnace went on, sending up a burrlike rattle.

"I still have it, Elaine. It's what you call . . . it's disintegrating. From the years. I want to keep them a few years more. Do you understand why, Elaine?"

"Yes, Olga," Elaine said softly. "I think I understand."

"That is a patch from them you are holding. I want you to match the fabric and bring me back enough to mend them with. I've looked, but I can't find the right color. None of the material I try seems to match. I look at the patch, and it's like it's mocking me. Like it's saying that even after lasting through all the camps and my family dying, it can't survive after all. I need your help, Elaine."

While Olga talked, Elaine had sat there with the piece of fabric on her lap next to her pocketbook, the top open just wide enough for her to see the major's seed, half-buried in tissue. She had planned to give it to Olga. She hadn't come for any new burdens. She knew exactly what she should say to her, if only she had the nerve:"Olga, I can't. Please don't ask me. I don't want it. I don't even want to look at it. It scratches my fingers. I'm done with things like that, Olga. It's not fair of you to ask."

"You take it home with you," Olga said. "You find something

the right color, and I'll mend it good as new. There's no hurry. You take your time."

She watched until Elaine had placed the fabric inside her pocketbook. As she led the way back through the hall, she changed the subject to Katya again.

"Poor Katya. The veterinarian wasn't very helpful. 'She's too sick,' he said. 'We must do away with her at once.' But I wouldn't let him. I took her home and nursed her back to health all by myself."

"Olga, I . . ."

Olga was shaking her head slowly back and forth. There were tears in her eyes, as if the horror of it had just struck her for the first time. "Can you imagine? If she hadn't been rescued at the last moment, they were going to destroy her. Imagine! This poor little thing. This innocent. A whole wonderful life ahead of her, and what happened? They were going to take this beautiful dreamy creature who never harmed a soul in the world and put her inside an oven!"

As soon as she got home, Elaine went into the workshop and locked the fabric away in the cabinet with the major's flower. She didn't want to look at either of them. She didn't want to think about old battles or concentration camps or dead sons, not for a while, not until she managed to catch her breath.

She took her coat off and sat down by her desk, trying to find enough strength to go upstairs. From habit, she turned on the answering machine to see if anyone had called while she was out.

Mr. Powers's voice came on, vibrating so much that at first she thought it must be due to a faulty tape.

"What was that crack about giving John up?"

There was nothing else to the message. A woman selling insulation came on next, then Mrs. Peabody, apologizing for what seemed the hundredth time about letting her mother escape. Elaine was reaching over to turn down the volume when Mr. Powers's voice came on again. Its calmness startled her even more than the anger had.

"Sorry for barking at you, Elaine, but I've been thinking it over, and you're absolutely right about wanting to get away from him for a while. May I make a suggestion? Why not come out to the Vineyard with us next month? We haven't used the place very much the last few years, but lately Carol's been talking about how nice it would be to spend a few weeks there, and we thought you might like to join us for a few days. You don't have to give me a yes or no right now. I just wanted to let you know the offer's there if you ever need it."

Elaine switched the rewind button to play it back, but changed her mind before she found the place in the tape where his message began. The major's funeral, Olga's fabric . . . she wasn't in the mood to make any decisions. She unhooked the machine and pushed the button on the phone that automatically transferred the calls upstairs.

"Hello, Mother."

"Hello, Elaine."

Mrs. Collier was sitting on the couch as she always did on Sundays, hands folded penitentially on her lap, eyeglasses low on her nose so she could see the screen without lifting her head. She had probably been sitting there ever since Elaine left, patiently waiting for the films to begin.

"It was such a lovely service today, Elaine. I saw Mr. Petrie, the butcher, in the next pew."

"Mr. Petrie is dead, Mother. Someone stabbed him for his wallet last May."

"He was talking to that nice young Robinson boy you go out with. He's really quite handsome, Elaine."

"He got married ten years ago, Mommy. His wife's an alcoholic."

Elaine was tired—tired from her day, tired from the constant struggle to understand her mother's fantasies without being dragged down with her into the soothing realm of Miller's Hash Heaven where long-dead friends appeared in the glistening reflections on the refrigerater door. But there was no getting out of it, not tonight. If she was to persuade her mother to eat supper, they would have to go through the inevitable motions of a Sunday evening—the films, the make-believe strollers, the final struggle to get her to bed.

She reached into the box for a film she had just finished working on and threaded it through the projector. Before she had spliced it with the Powers's film, it had been one of their oldest and emptiest: Elaine playing by herself in the sand at Coney Island the summer she was ten.

"Can you see, Mommy?"

"Fine, my love."

There was a slight hesitation as the splice went through, then several blank frames where her mother—on the boardwalk looking down at her—had stumbled in aiming the camera. After swerving past seagulls and strollers and lifeguards, the camera finally managed to focus on the sand. There on the empty beach with Elaine was a handsome boy her own age, much browner than she was, looking out toward a greenish blue sea specked with triangular sails. She sat staring off to the other side of the screen where there was another sea, this one gray and cold-looking. He was fiddling with a dial on a scuba tank; she was digging grimly at the dirty sand near her knees with a metal shovel.

"Oh, look, Mommy!" Elaine said, deliberately mocking her own childish voice. "Do you remember who that is?"

Her mother propped herself up on the cushion for a better look. She squinted, then gave Elaine the scornful, condescending look senile people save for lucid intervals when they've caught someone humoring them with a foolish question.

"Why of course I do, my love," she whispered. "It's John. It's my son John."

"What?"

Mrs. Collier sneezed.

"What did you say?" Elaine demanded.

"Gesundheit."

"No, *before* you sneezed. About John."

"John?"

Elaine was so startled that she forgot to turn off the projector. The end of the film snapped out of the viewfinder and started spilling off the reel. Everything was total confusion after that. Elaine made a clumsy grab for the off switch and knocked the projector over, her mother started crying, uncoiled ribbons of film writhed madly across the floor, the projector's bulb shattered, sparks flew out from the plug.

"It's all right, Mommy," Elaine said, trying to calm her down and find the light switch at the same time. "It's all right!"

When Elaine finally managed to get the lights on, her mother lay curled up on the couch with her face buried in the pillow as if a bomb had gone off. Elaine knelt on the carpet next to her and started to stroke her hair.

"It's only a splice I put in, Mommy. Our movies are so choppy, I thought I'd add new film. Just to fill up the empty spots. There's this boy I'm working on. He's . . ."

But she might as well have been talking Greek. Even before she finished, she realized that she would have to find another way of accounting for him before things got out of hand.

"John was my friend," she insisted. "My *friend*, Mommy. Just my friend. Remember him? Remember that little boy?"

Mrs. Collier stopped sobbing. She sat up and looked attentively at the dark screen as if she still saw something there.

"With blond hair?" she sniffed. "Taller than you?"

"That's right," Elaine said encouragingly. "Remember him? My *friend*. He used to live down the street. You used to take movies of us playing."

"In the park?"

"Yes. My friend John. He was a nice boy, Mommy."

"Oh, he was, Elaine. You used to look so happy together. You were such good friends." She suddenly looked troubled. "Elaine? Can I ask you something?"

"What?"

"Will dinner be ready soon?"

Elaine almost laughed out loud from relief. "Yes, Mommy. I think it's ready now. Shall we go and see?"

It serves me right for playing with her memory like that, Elaine told herself. But luckily her mother didn't mention him again during dinner. If anything, she seemed happier and calmer than usual; for once, Elaine didn't have to remind her to eat what was on her fork. Elaine knew from experience that the only way to talk her mother out of a delusion was to do it the moment it first formed. She felt grateful at having nipped this latest one before it could get out of hand, but she thought it would be a good idea to get her mother's mind on someone else.

"Did the Reverend Thomas give an interesting sermon this morning?" she asked as she cleared their plates.

"Oh, yes!"

Smiling, her eyes half shut in pleasure, Mrs. Collier began to tell Elaine about her day.

There was a third beach, halfway between the other two. Elaine walked along it as the sun came up, letting the foam cover her bare toes, reaching down to turn over a shell the tide had brought in. The shoreline curved here. It was difficult to see where the beach started or where it led. Squinting, shading her eyes, she could just make out the first curl of dune behind her, poised high above the house like a breaker about to crash. She stood for a moment as if expecting someone to come out. No one did. She knelt down and drew an arrow in the sand, then started up the beach in the direction it pointed.

She was alone for only a short while. But brief as it was, the walk provided her with an extraordinarily vivid memory, one that didn't seem tied to any definite place or particular time. Later, she found she could place it at several alternate points in her life that were otherwise vacant. She could imagine herself a lonely little girl playing tag with the rushing surf. She could imagine herself a serious teenager seeking enlightenment from the sea. She could, most vividly of all, imagine herself a confused woman of thirty-five, trying to sort out her feelings before going back to the house. But wherever she put it, no matter how many retrospective fantasies she might later build, the beach itself couldn't be manipulated or spliced or discarded or changed. It was a real beach she was walking on, a beach she could see and touch and smell.

Ahead of her was a surf fisherman, knee-deep in the sea. When he cast, the sun spun off his wet, arcing line in rainbows. When he reeled in, he seemed like a giant towing in the surf.

As she stood there watching, he hooked a fish. It was a large one judging by the way the rod curved. The man was pulled farther out, and he was up to his waist before he managed to check the fish's run. It was a seesaw after that. At times it appeared the fish was winning; at times the fisherman had regained most of his line. Her sympathy swayed both ways. She imagined the fish racing in panic from the constant tugging of an unknown force. Then, just as quickly, she felt herself the fisherman, the strain coming not in the mouth but in the hands and arms, patiently, deliberately, coaxing a mystery in to where it could be solved.

She wasn't sure how long it lasted. Ten minutes, twenty at the most. The fish shot out of the water much farther offshore than she had guessed it could be, cartwheeling joyously over in spray before splashing back in. The fisherman yelled—she saw his line snap in midair, severing the rainbow. At the same time, a rogue wave higher than the others cascaded against her body, drenching her, stinging her eyes, making her giddy, almost knocking her down. Turning to keep her balance, she saw another man coming toward her: Mr. Powers, though at first she didn't recognize him. The sun was at his back, his features were indistinct in the glare, and for one blinding moment she was able to turn his image into any of the men she had needed so badly in her life—father, brother, lover, friend; a strong, faceless, compassionate man walking through the surf to take her hand and lead her safely back to shore.

It was the potential for experiences like this that had finally made Elaine accept Mr. Powers's invitation to Martha's Vineyard. "I need the chance to get away," she told him on the phone, echoing his own argument. "I think the change will do me good." But true as these reasons were, they hid an even deeper reason that she didn't try to explain: she desperately needed new memories, as many as her imagination would hold. Sunrises, the dizzy sensation of sand racing away beneath her heels, souvenir pebbles and shells . . . she would go to the island and stock up her empty past with these in the same way she had longed to stock up the empty toy chest in her room as a little girl. This will be my escape, she decided after she hung up. This will be the moment when I start leading my own life again, with friends and adventures my mother can't share.

Olga had volunteered to stay with her mother while Elaine was gone. She came over to the house for dinner the first week in June, and she and Mrs. Collier hit it off right from the start.

"Why, hello, Louise!" she said when Olga came in. "Long time no see!"

Olga didn't even blink.

"Hello yourself, stranger," she replied, taking her by the arm like a long-lost friend. "Why don't we sit on the couch here and talk over old times while Elaine fixes us supper."

Elaine could have hugged her for that. The entire evening went by in the same vein, Mrs. Collier rattling on about Louise and her other cousins, Olga patiently listening. By the time Olga left around nine, it was all arranged.

"I need a change of air myself," Olga admitted. "It's not the same in the house with the general away. I'll pack a suitcase and Katya can bring her dish."

She arrived bright and early the morning Elaine was due to leave, Katya's travel box in one hand, a bag of kitty litter in the other. Elaine gave her the Powers's Vineyard number in case anything went wrong and explained about the notes on the refrigerator and the shopping expeditions through the hall.

"You go ahead to Margaret's whatever-you-call-it," Olga said, shooing her toward the door. "Mommy and I are going out dancing, maybe meet a couple of nice men, who knows?"

"I'm positive that I've forgotten something. I told you about the locks on the door, didn't I? You'll remember about the egg salad?"

Olga laughed. "There's the doorbell. Go!"

The drive up was embarrassing, at least to Elaine. Mrs. Powers sat in the back seat, insisting Elaine sit in front with Mr. Powers. Elaine twisted sideways so that she could talk to both of them, but it was no use. Mrs. Powers seemed to have deteriorated since she had last seen her. She was dressed as expensively as ever, her hair was just as perfectly arranged, but there was something confused and precious about the way she talked, as though her mind had suddenly turned senile.

"It's so good of you to come, Elaine," she said. "Richard's told me so much about you. I insist you think of yourself as a member of our family. Just the three of us, won't that be fun?"

"Don't forget Roddy Martins," Mr. Powers said, slowing down to pay a toll. "Fred and Linda said something about dropping by, too. They're having a clambake tomorrow night on their beach. I'm afraid we're invited."

"Clams?" Mrs. Powers asked. "Did I hear someone mention clams?"

"Yes, dear," he answered, glancing over at Elaine. "Clams."

But it was on the subject of John that the change was most noticeable. After a few preliminary attempts at politeness, Mrs. Powers talked about him nonstop for the entire drive. At times she described him in great detail, leaving out nothing, not even the painful episodes she was supposedly in the process of forgetting. Seconds later, she changed completely, becoming vague, breaking off in midsentence, as if encountering a protective blank in her stream of recollection. In the first instance she talked about John without any visible emotion at all, as though he were a chance acquaintance. In the second, it was very definitely her son she was describing, with great gusts of maternal affection, even sobs, but with no details, no conclusions to attach her emotions to. She was either exact and indifferent, or vague and caring, but no matter how long she talked she never quite managed to synchronize the proper feeling with the proper John.

Elaine asked Mr. Powers about this when they had stopped for coffee, while they were waiting for Mrs. Powers to come back from the rest room. Mr. Powers didn't seem particularly concerned.

"It's just part of the process of forgetting him," he said blandly. "I wouldn't worry about it if I were you."

"But I feel I'm responsible."

"You are. For helping her. It's just the scar tissue you're seeing, that's all."

They reached the ferry a half-hour before it was due to sail. Mr. Powers went to the package store to buy some vodka; Elaine found a drugstore that sold post cards. The ferry ride itself didn't take very long. Mrs. Powers stayed below in the car while Mr. Powers took Elaine to the top deck and pointed out the various lighthouses.

Behind them was a family feeding the seagulls popcorn. The parents had on matching sweat shirts from an amusement park in Canada; the children talked in a language Elaine couldn't quite pin down. The gulls hovered over the rail, darting in to take the kernels from their hands. Though the birds were performing miracles of aerodynamics to remain in place by the rail, though looking at the delight of the smallest girl made Elaine want to laugh along with her, no one else on the top deck seemed to notice the scene.

Finally, just before the ferry swung in toward land, one of the boys was bitten by a gull either clumsier or greedier than the rest. The boy screamed. The blood ran down his arm, his parents started shouting in Russian or Polish, first at the bird, then at the child. Mr. Powers, after looking around the deck to see if anyone else was going to help, reluctantly went over and ushered the screaming boy and his parents down below for first aid.

"Day trippers," he said when he got back.

"What's that supposed to mean?" Elaine demanded. "Is he seriously hurt?"

"How do I know? The lady behind the lunch counter took him off my hands. Let's enjoy the scenery, shall we?"

It was then that Elaine realized that he had helped only because he wanted to remove the crude, out-of-place show of pain from sight. The difference between those who belonged and those who didn't went much deeper than indifference to seagulls. The real distinction was in the ruthlessness of those who lounged around the top deck toward suffering of even a minor kind, their determination to ban it from their ferry and their island and their weekend, as if by a special zoning code less affluent citizens could be forced to ache and bleed in neighborhoods far away from them. There were two kinds of people in the world, Elaine decided: those who experienced pain, and those who, through money or luck or cheating, didn't, and the men and women sitting around her would do anything to convince themselves they were divinely placed in the latter group. Like Mr. Powers, they would all be good in minor emergencies. Like Mr. Powers, they could be counted on to take charge, see that whoever was injured was taken away promptly. *Away*, that was the important word. Once the wounded were invisible, their concern would end. For the first time it occurred to her that perhaps Mr. Powers had another reason for wanting to be rid of John than the one he had told her. It was only a question at this stage, a small doubt in the back of her mind. She knew now she needed more information on the relationship between father and son.

"There's East Chop," he said. "Won't be long now."

A crowd of people was waiting for the ferry when it docked. Men waved fishing rods at one another, women embraced, guests were sorted out and led to the appropriate station wagons. Mr. Powers, who knew each of the deck hands by name, managed to get their car off first, giving them a head start on the traffic leaving town.

The Powers's house faced the ocean. It wasn't as large as Elaine had pictured it. There were only two bedrooms, a small living room and a sundeck overlooking the water. The lavishness was in the furnishings and decorations: antiques, oil paintings, mobiles. Elaine thought it was more like a gallery than a house, a space not for people, but for things.

Mrs. Powers took her to the guest room. She unpacked slowly, trying to sort out her feelings before going downstarirs. From her window she could see sailboats tilted sideways on the horizon, tacking back and forth on the same parallel course, and, closer to the house, someone standing alone on the beach watching them with binoculars. It was Mr. Powers. He had changed into jeans. It made him seem much younger, and the arrogance of the ferry was gone. There was something wistful about the way he stared at the distant boats.

Downstairs, Mrs. Powers was setting the table. "There you are! All unpacked?"

"It's a beautiful room, Mrs. Powers. Can I help you with something?"

"Call me Carol, dear. But yes, isn't it? We had it painted that shade years ago. I was afraid at first the yellow might be a bit too . . . too vegetable. Richard used to claim it was the color of summer squash. But we like it now."

"I've never seen such a lovely view," Elaine said, sitting down on a stool near the window. "You and Mr. Powers must really love it here."

"Richard must really love what?" she echoed vaguely.

He was coming inside now, stamping his sneakers on the door-mat to get off the sand.

"Have you two ladies been talking about the master of the house in his absence?" he asked.

"Oh, there you are, darling! Elaine was just telling me how much she likes the yellow. A young man painted it for us years ago. A very nice young man. I remember him sitting there on a bucket of paint in the middle of the room wondering exactly where to start. He'd plot it all out first, you see, just as if he was doing a portrait or a mural: what corner to paint first and so on. It was quite a science. Once he started, there was no stopping him. I never saw anyone work so hard."

"Don't you think it's time we were eating, Carol?"

"I remember he came down here once he was done, absolutely covered with paint. 'Why you look a mess!' I told him. And do you know what he did? He ran outside in his overalls and jumped into the ocean, all because I said he looked a mess. Just to make me laugh. He was always doing things like that. Remember that boy, Richard? I understand that later on he was killed."

"It was blue paint," Mr. Powers said, staring at his wife the way he had stared at the sailboats. "We had it painted yellow last year. *Last* year. There was no boy."

"The nicest shade of yellow," Mrs. Powers continued. "I remember the way it looked in his hair. Blond, only blonder."

Mr. Powers shrugged. "Blond. You're absolutely right. Now, don't you think it's time for dinner? Elaine will think we're barbarians eating so early, but . . . do you mind, Elaine?"

"I'm famished," she said, picking up her cue. "It must be the salt air."

They ate on the sundeck. Elaine was surprised to find that as long as the conversation stayed off young men, Mrs. Powers could be an animated, responsive woman. She described all their neighbors in great detail, making Elaine laugh with her imitations. Mr. Powers, cheering up perceptibly at this change in his wife, trotted out his own party piece: an imitation of a New England lobsterman visiting New York for the first time. The moon came up while they talked. Mr. Powers spilled the charcoal from the hibachi onto the beach, and the briquettes flared up like miniature meteorites before they fell into the sand.

"Richard! You're polluting again."

"Nonsense. I'll clean it up in the morning."

Mrs. Powers excused herself the moment they had finished dessert, saying it had gotten so dark she must go find a lamp. But when she came back moments later, she was carrying a tennis racket.

"This is my son John's, Elaine. He used to play every afternoon when he was small. We bought it for him on his birthday. His twelfth birthday, I believe. We bought it for him when he went away to school."

She walked toward the edge of the deck, holding it rigidly in front of her body like a crucifix. There was a hallucinatory quality in the way she stared, which, in the dark, reminded Elaine of a roommate she had once had who was subject to epileptic attacks that changed her entire personality in seconds.

"But he left us, you know. He wrote us a letter. Then we received another letter, but it wasn't from him." Mrs. Powers started crying.

Elaine started over to her, but Mr. Powers got there first, taking her by the hand and leading her quickly inside, the same way he had taken the boy down below on the ferry. When he came back, alone, he made a half-hearted attempt to pretend nothing had happened.

"Sorry about that, Elaine," he said. "Now, where was I? Did I get to the part where the lobsterman goes into a seafood restaurant on Forty-second Street and sees . . ."

"Richard . . ."

He took her hand before she could say anything more. "No, listen, I want to explain something to you, only not here. Let's go into the kitchen where it's warmer. I'll make some coffee."

The pity that Elaine felt toward him had come back the moment she saw him staring in dismay at his wife. It was even stronger now that they were alone. She found herself wanting to comfort him but not sure how, afraid that she would say the wrong thing and make it worse.

"Carol's much better now," he said, sitting down across from her. "Sometimes I think she's gotten over him entirely. Then out of the blue something like this happens. But in a way I'm glad you saw it. Now you know exactly what I'm up against."

"She's a beautiful woman," Elaine said. "They must have been very close to each other. Do you think I should go and see if she's all right?"

"Beautiful's not the word. I only wish you could have known her before anything went wrong. She was so vivacious. So strong. Did she tell you how we met? It was in 1945. I'd just gotten my commission in the Navy, and there was a party for us in Boston. We knew the war was almost over, but we figured it might pay off later on having been in, even for a month or two. There I was, a few months out of college, feeling awkward in my uniform, wondering how long I had to stay before I could duck out, when I saw this girl—she couldn't have been much over eighteen—standing all by herself near the door. I knew the moment I saw her she was the most beautiful thing I'd ever seen. And I knew I wanted her, too. Don't give up the ship, Powers, I told myself. I took a deep breath and went over to her. Turned out we had friends in common. Her brother was on destroyers, her roommate knew mine. Before the week was out, we were engaged. I didn't see her for two months after that. It was pretty tough on us both. The ship I was on was decommissioned in New York, and her father sent the limousine down for me. We were married two weeks later. Nine months after that John was born."

"In 1946."

"Yes. I wish to hell now it had been 1956. Having a teenage son in the seventies would have been child's play compared to what we went through."

He pointed at the tennis racket in the corner. "We bought that for him the summer he won the club juniors. Above the refrigerator is a painting he did in college. You're sleeping in his bed. He painted the house his sophomore year. The chair you're sitting on was his favorite chair. In the closet behind you is his lacrosse stick. Tomorrow we'll go sailing in his boat."

He said it fast, in one brutal rush. Elaine got up to turn off the coffee before it boiled over. When she came back, he was sitting hunched over on the chair, his head in his hands.

"I think I can forgive him everything except that," he whispered. "Ruining her. Destroying her. All the things he did to me were minor compared to that. I'd give anything, *anything,* to have her back again the way she was."

His vehemence frightened Elaine. He looked at her without seeing—he had the expression of a man who wants to hit something but isn't sure what.

"*Anything . . .*"

He was shaking his head, pulling himself together with the same act of will she had seen him use in handing back John's toy airplane the first afternoon in her office. A moment more and he had regained his habitual mask of self-control, but he put it in place a bit too abruptly this time, as if he had inadvertently revealed to her something that she hadn't been meant to see.

"Enough of that," he said apologetically. "I'd kill for a drink right about now. There's an interesting little place in town. Care to try it?"

It was too sudden for her, the switch in tone, the casual assumption that she would go along with the invitation. She heard herself refusing him, but more from reflex than anything—even as she told him no, she wanted him to ask her again, wanted him to coax her out of all her doubts and hesitations just as Peter had on that spring afternoon long ago.

"Thanks, but may I have a rain check? I have my heart set on seeing the sunrise, and if I don't get to bed soon I'll never make it."

She wasn't sure, but she thought his shoulders slumped a bit at this, the way a tense person's will when he suddenly feels relieved.

"That's too bad," he said.

"Would we be getting back very late?"

"Yes."

He carried their cups over to the sink and turned on the tap.

"I'm sorry to be such a killjoy," she said without getting up. "Maybe tomorrow night?"

"Tomorrow night's the famous clambake. I have no idea when it will end. But that's okay. Go to bed and get a good night's rest. I'm going for a walk."

"By yourself?"

"I'm not tired yet."

"I'll go if you want me to."

"Don't be silly. I need the exercise. Know your way upstairs?"

"I'll find it."

"Great. Goodnight then."

"Goodnight. Richard?"

"Yes, ma'am?"

"Thank you for a wonderful day."

He laughed. "Thank *you.* Sweet dreams."

Elaine set the alarm for five, but she was awake before it went off. She tiptoed down the stairs, quietly unlatched the kitchen door and started across the sand toward the water. Later, she wasn't sure whether both of the Powers had heard her leave and followed her together, or whether each had come on his own. All she knew was that when Mr. Powers led her back to shore after the wave hit her, Mrs. Powers was waiting with a terry-cloth towel.

"You must be freezing," she said, folding it over Elaine's shoulders. "We followed your arrow."

"I was just watching that fisherman over there," Elaine said. She turned to point him out, but there was no sign of either fisherman or fish. The sun had gone behind a cloud. For a moment she wondered if she had invented the entire scene.

"It was probably Jack Keys," Mr. Powers said reassuringly. "He's a fanatic when it comes to surf casting." He pointed toward the house. "Carol and I are driving into town for supplies. You're welcome to come along if you'd like."

He said it rather half-heartedly. Elaine decided to say no.

"Is there any coffee left?" she asked. "I'd like to spend the morning here on the beach if that's all right."

The three of them walked back toward the house together, the Powers branching off once they reached the driveway. Elaine fixed herself breakfast, then went back out to the beach and found a spot near the jetty where there was shade if she wanted it. She spread the towel carefully across the sand, smoothing out the bumps, anchoring the ends with suntan lotion and magazines. She was lying there on her back, eyes closed, enjoying the mind-less tranquillity sun brings, when she felt something cool cross her cheek, leave, then come back. It's another cloud, she thought. But when she opened her eyes it turned out to be a man's shadow. A man her own age was standing looking down at her with a smile on his face. She sat up quickly.

"You're Elaine, right?"

"Right."

"You're staying with Dick and Carol, right?"

"Right."

"My name is Rod Martins, how are you?"

"Fine."

He sat down on the sand next to her.

"I guess I should explain," he said. "I'm your officially desig-nated escort for the clambake tonight. At least I *was*. That's what I should explain. I've got to take the boat back to the mainland this afternoon. Training session for the new men on Monday I've got to get ready for. Very serious stuff. Carol invited me. Pisces, right? That's what she said. I saw them in town, so I thought I'd come out and break the tragic news in person. Dick said to keep walking until I found a woman who'd forgotten how pretty she was and that would be you."

Elaine smiled. "Do you live in Boston?"

"Sometimes." He looked at his watch. "We have exactly twenty . . . make that nineteen minutes to talk. Where shall we start? Mutual friends, don't you think? Always start off a conversation with mutual friends. Have you known the Powers long?"

"Not long. You?"

"For years. My parents are very close, et cetera. Golf club, yacht club, club club. John's the one I was close to. At least as close as he let anyone get. Did you know John?"

She didn't answer him, not directly. "You're the boy who tried to keep him from falling off the sailboat," she said, suddenly remembering where she had seen his features before. "I saw a picture of the two of you," she added when he looked puzzled.

"That's not surprising," he said. "There must be thousands of pictures of John lying around. John Powers, the All-American boy. That's what we used to call him. Not John. Not All-American. It had to be John-Powers-the-All-American-boy, and we'd say it just like that, fast as we could. And not sarcastically either. He fit the role. The guy could do anything. Sports, school . . . he was so clearly the best at everything none of us even bothered getting jealous. It's funny how it turned out."

"Funny?"

"Him getting killed in 'Nam."

He abruptly started telling her about his job in Boston, making fun of his own aspirations in a way that couldn't hide the fact that he felt superfluous and trapped. He jogged, he said. He'd been married twice, but neither time had worked out.

"You know what's strange, Elaine? When you actually think about it I mean? All the potential I had when I was a kid. Where did it go? I mean sometimes I get really down on myself, but then I think what in hell was I supposed to do? We grew up, we studied and exercised, we were all set for the challenge, and then they pulled a fast one on us. There *was* no challenge. Not a goddamn one. Selling more bonds, teaching Renaissance English. Call those challenges? That's what's funny about John. I can't imagine him doing what I'm doing, running laps around reservoirs, going to an office all day. It may sound terrible, but it's probably just as well he was killed. Sometimes I think I should have been, too. Sometimes I think I was. Right around my twenty-third birthday. Shot down in mid-air, been buried ever since."

He glanced down at his watch.

"Oh, God! There goes my ferry! It's been fun, Elaine. Sorry about tonight. You coming out here again?"

"Not that I know of."

He took out a pen and wrote his phone number down on the cover of one of her magazines. "If you're ever in Boston, et cetera."

"Sure. If you're ever in New York . . ."

"Super!"

He brushed the sand off his pants and started running toward the parking lot. About halfway there he stopped and turned around. "Did you know John got kicked out of college?" he yelled.

"No!" Elaine called back. "Why?"

"For making a snowman! See you around!"

She found it difficult to relax after he left. She went into the water for a while, then walked along the outermost edge of the sand, stopping to admire sand castles children were building, occasionally lending a hand with a flooded wall. When she got back to the towel, Mr. Powers was there. He was wearing trunks, and he'd brought an umbrella, which he was jabbing into the sand in a way that displayed his broad chest and strong arms.

"Hello!" Mrs. Powers called, carrying a picnic basket across the sand. "Guess what I've brought."

Mr. Powers went in the ocean after lunch. Mrs. Powers went to talk to some friends farther down the beach. Apparently he had been waiting for this; he came back the moment she left.

"Enjoying yourself?"

"If you ask me that one more time I'm going to *scream*."

He laughed. "Only checking."

"I was just talking to the nicest person, Rod Martins. He wanted to apologize for not being able to make the party tonight. He said he was going to be my date."

Mr. Powers looked embarrassed. "Well, it *seemed* like a good idea at the time."

"He talked quite a bit about John."

"John? That's natural enough, I suppose. Once upon a time they were good friends. Roddy's a fine young man. Doing quite well for himself these days, too. Just got a nice promotion from what Rod Senior tells me. He's a credit to them both."

He turned away and looked off toward the lifeguard, who was blowing his whistle at someone who had swum out too far.

"About last night, Elaine. I didn't mean to sound so . . . so negative about John. We had a good relationship, all things considered. When he was young, there wasn't anything I wouldn't do for him. It wasn't until he went to college that things changed. After that it was as if he were a different person. I remember thinking once that the John we raised had committed suicide and left someone else who looked and talked just like him but acted completely different. It was as if he weren't our son any more . . . The reason I get upset is because things were going so well for all of us, and then he had to go and deliberately involve me in it."

"Involve you in what?"

"The sixties. All the garbage that went with it. I remember I used to watch the news at night and thank God it had nothing to do with me. Then all of a sudden it did. I had a son in the army. I had a boy caught up in all the sordidness and filth. I couldn't stand the thought that John had allowed himself to get trapped like that, as if his parents were poor white trash. Except for him, I could have ridden the decade out without dirtying my hands at all . . . Toward the end of 1968 demonstrators picketed my office saying I was a war criminal because of our defense contracts. Defense contracts, okay? You know what we built? The suspensions for field ambulances. Twenty measly tons of steel a year. Nowadays, people talk as if the sixties were some fantastic, stimulating time. Bullshit! We'd be better off without them. You could go right from 1959 to 1970 and no one would know the difference."

"I still don't understand," Elaine said. "Why do you feel guilty? You didn't force John to go."

"Who feels guilty?"

"You do. Why else would you want to disown him like this?"

"Wait a second, Elaine. You've got it backward. It was John who did the disowning. He washed his hands of us as parents. So why shouldn't I wash my hands of him as a son?"

"What do you mean?"

"Never mind. Now that I'm dried off, I need another swim. Coming?"

She would have liked to stay on the beach all day, but after their swim, he dragged her off to go for a sail on their boat, to shop, sightsee—there wasn't any letup in the schedule until they got back to the house around six, and even then there was the clambake to get ready for. Elaine took a quick shower, put on clean jeans and fixed her hair as best she could. When she came downstairs, Mr. Powers was mixing her a drink.

"Just in time for a Powers' special," he said.

"Will I have time to drink it?"

He didn't catch her irony. "Sure," he said. "Carol won't be ready for at least another half-hour."

He handed the glass to her on a coaster. "Ever been to a clambake, Elaine? This local character named Bourne is going to be bake master. His family's been doing it for years."

"That's nice."

She pointed to the phone on the end table. "Do you mind if I call home? I think I'd enjoy myself a lot more tonight if I did."

"Of course. Here, let me get out of your way. Make sure you dial one first."

"You don't have to leave."

"Nonsense. It's time I got dressed."

There were all kinds of clicks and buzzing sounds over the line before the call went through. It made Elaine feel even farther away from home than she really was.

"Hello? Who is this calling, please?"

Olga apparently believed in answering the phone in the same cautious way she answered her doorbell.

"It's Elaine, Olga."

"Oh, hello Elaine," she said, speaking much louder. "Are you having a good time?"

"Yes and no, Olga. Mostly yes though. I sent you a post card this afternoon. How is everything there?"

"Did you go into the ocean?"

"It was perfect, just the right temperature. Is my mother all right?"

"How about fishing? Did you go fishing?"

"No, Olga. Olga?"

"Hello! Yes, I'm still here. Did you catch any fish?"

"I didn't go fishing. Listen, is everything okay?"

"They have tuna fish there, don't they?"

"I suppose so. You're not trying to hide anything from me, are you?"

Elaine didn't have to wait for her answer to know something was wrong. The forced nonchalance in Olga's voice reminded her of the phone call she had received in Boston from her Aunt Carrie fifteen years ago, the call that told her her mother had set fire to the house. Carrie had been careful to break the news gently, too, asking Elaine about her classes and friends first, as if nothing were wrong. Elaine remembered this as the most frightening part of the entire nightmare: Carrie's calm voice, her own growing certainty that it masked some disaster, the terrible time she'd had making Carrie admit it.

"What's wrong, Olga?" Elaine demanded. "Tell me!"

"There is nothing to become worried about."

"She's not hurt, is she?"

"Oh, no. Your mother is one healthy cookie."

"Where is she? Did she get out again?"

"She is curled up on the kitchen floor like a church mouse."

"On the floor!"

Just as Carrie had, Olga dropped her pretense all at once.

"She is crying, Elaine. Ever since you left. I tried to call you all day, no one answered."

"Crying about me? I told her I'd be back soon. She never . . ."

"About your brother John."

Elaine didn't respond at first. There was a moment when she felt something like panic, but it passed so quickly that she later wondered if she hadn't been expecting her mother to do this all along. It was the other half of her, the calm, professional half, that answered Olga, just as it had answered Aunt Carrie years before.

"Listen to me very carefully, Olga. It's another delusion of hers. I have no brother. I never had a brother."

"But she's been telling me about him all day," Olga insisted. "She's going around looking for a picture to show me. That's when she started crying, because she couldn't find it. I think she is becoming hysterical. Is there a doctor I can call?"

It was the sudden quiver in Olga's voice that worried Elaine most. Olga was not the kind of person to get upset over nothing.

"No, Olga. A doctor won't help anyway."

"Is there a pill she can swallow?"

"Humor her, Olga. Listen to her, ask her questions about him. I'll get a bus home tomorrow as early as I can."

"She's ripping the closets apart looking for something. She won't tell me for what."

"She's looking for him, Olga. Hear me? For *him.* You'll have to let her find what she's looking for, there's no other cure. Go downstairs to my workshop. There's a brown folder on my desk. If it's not there, then it's on my work table. It says 'John Powers' on the outside. In it are some letters. Take one out and give it to my mother. Understand? Tell her it's from John."

Elaine made Olga repeat the instructions back to her to make sure she had them right.

"I'll be home as soon as I can, Olga. I'll call you when I know when."

"She thinks you are bringing him home souvenirs, Elaine. That's all she keeps talking about."

"I'll pick up a T-shirt or something on the ferry."

"What if she asks where he is?"

"Tell her he's away at college, but only if you have to. I'll be home tomorrow afternoon at the latest."

Elaine's steadiness seemed to have its effect on Olga. She sounded much calmer by the time Elaine hung up, but it was the kind of transfusion that leaves the donor drained. Elaine ran toward the stairs feeling the worry flood back in a wave.

"Whoa there," Mr. Powers said playfully, stepping in front of her in the hall. "Where's the fire?"

"My mother's sick. I'm going home."

"Don't be silly. You're staying all week."

"She's sick. She's having some sort of breakdown."

"What else is new?" he said sarcastically. "Don't you think it's time you faced facts and put her in an institution?"

It was all Elaine needed.

"Why don't you put your wife in an institution!" she said, her voice rising in anger. "That's your solutiion for everything, isn't it? Get rid of everybody that suffers, drag them away! It must be nice living in a world of contented rich people, Richard. How much does it cost? I mean to dispose of the unhappy ones that way."

"You don't have to take it out on me, Elaine," Mr. Powers said gently.

His patience only made her angrier. "What happens when you start getting old and senile, Richard, and somebody decides to shut you away? It won't be long now, you know. I can already see it in your face."

She wasn't sure why she wanted to hurt him so, whether it was his remark about her mother, the tension she had felt between them on the beach that afternoon, or her need to disassociate herself from his world and everyone in it. She thought later that it might have been solely for the satisfaction of seeing him lose his temper and yell back.

It didn't work. Instead of yelling, he reached for the phone.

"There's a flight to La Guardia at eight," he said. "It's probably full, but there's someone I can call. You'll be home by ten."

All Elaine's anger disappeared. She sat down on the couch.

"I'm sorry, Richard. I was snapping at life, not you."

He cupped his hand over the receiver. "That's okay," he said. "I know how concerned you are. Your mother's the important one right now. The Vineyard will still be here in August if you want to come back."

It didn't take him long to make the arrangements. Elaine hurried upstairs to pack, tucking the shells she had found on the beach inside her extra shoes, spreading her wet bathing suit on top of her robe. Mrs. Powers peeked in before she was done.

"I'm sorry about your bad news," she said. "I hope it's not the flu."

"Thank you," Elaine said distractedly. "I hope so, too."

Mr. Powers had the car running in the driveway. They dropped Mrs. Powers at the beach on the way to the airport. The clambake was in full swing—Elaine could see couples crossing the sand with their shoes in their hands. She couldn't see much else. A van was parked on her side of the car, and the view was about the same as it would have been if she were looking through a half-opened door. The party lights seemed like little points of color, stars seen through haze. The laughter and the music were absorbed by the sand before they could reach her.

It was Boston all over again—the being on the verge of a new life that was suddenly snatched away. But in one important respect it was completely different. Leaving Boston, she had been convinced that she was leaving all that was best about herself behind—her independence, her friends. She had been heartbroken; she had done everything in her power to come back. Leaving the Vineyard, all she felt was a kind of tranquil numbness. What did clambakes and sailboats have to do with her? She was going home where she belonged.

"She *needs* me," Elaine said to herself. She was going home to see her mother through this latest crisis, just as she had the first time. She had caused this one—it was up to her to see it through, no matter what direction it took. As before, she would have to find the patience to understand her mother's whims. As before, she would have to take her to the clinic, see to it that she wasn't left alone for very long. Elaine had been too rushed to give much thought to the phone call's implications, but now images of her mother raced through her head—her mother in the kitchen the day word came about her father, her mother alone at the nursing home on Staten Island, her mother smiling to see John in the film, her mother at her very best the rest of that night after she had seen him there. It was this last image that was most vivid now, and with it came a thought that wouldn't go away, no matter how confused and guilty it made her feel: *It would be easier this time; she would have John to help.*

It didn't take long to reach the airport. Mr. Powers checked her bags in, took her to the coffee shop, ordered her a sandwich and sat with her in the booth until it was time to board. Elaine had hardly been aware of him during the drive, but now that they were about to say good-by she found herself wanting to rest her head on his shoulder, feel him comfort her, have him put his arm around her and pull her closer. All the different emotions she had felt toward him in the past few months, all the longing and anger and pity, had coalesced into this one simple desire. She slid across the booth toward him. She tilted her head . . .

But it was no use. He sat an angle to her with his legs crossed, as if he had anticipated her gesture and secretly dreaded it, choosing just this posture as the one best calculated to keep her away.

"Richard, I'm cold," she said softly.

"Cold? Don't be ridiculous. It's the middle of July."

And as suddenly as that she didn't care any more, and all she could think about was getting home.

"What exactly is wrong with your mother?" he asked later, sensing her remoteness, trying too late to make up. "I know a few shrinks out here. Maybe one of them could help."

"I've already tried. They said it was because she wants a son."

"A son?" he said in disbelief, staring off into space. "I wish to God I'd never had one."

Neither of them said anything after that. He kissed her on the forehead at the gate, and when she turned around to wave goodby he was already gone.

 When she got home, there were signs of struggle everywhere. Milk was spilled over the kitchen table; the bedroom closets had been torn apart and a lamp knocked down in the hall. In her anxiety, Elaine rushed into the living room so fast that she nearly tripped over her mother, sprawled against the couch with Olga slumped at her feet and Katya pacing nervously over their legs as if standing guard. Olga had John's graduation picture in her right hand; her mother clutched one of his letters.

It was Olga who woke up first.

"Yes, he's a very nice boy," Olga mumbled.

She tried to push herself up, shook her head, shook it again, and was just about to go back to sleep again when she noticed Elaine.

"Your mother has him now," she said, without any preliminary. She handed Elaine the picture. "Is this him? I was saving it in case the letter wasn't enough."

Elaine helped her up. "You can sleep in my room tonight, Olga. We're all too tired to talk about it now."

But Olga was fully awake and asked Elaine to call a cab.

"Enough is enough. I'm getting too old to baby-sit, Elaine. She is all yours."

"I won't forget your help, Olga. I haven't had time yet to match your fabric, but as soon as my mother calms down . . ."

"You take your time, Elaine. Me, I just want to get home."

Elaine waited out in front with her until the cab came. When she got back to the living room, her mother was still asleep. Elaine decided to leave her there; she was too exhausted to try to wrestle her into bed. She gently pried the letter from her hand and searched underneath the couch until she found the folder that held the rest. She hadn't read any of them yet—there had been the films and photographs to work on first, and they hadn't seemed particularly important, at least up to now. But if she was going to let her mother read them, she would have to read them, too, at the very least to know what her mother was talking about. But there was another reason: the trip to the Vineyard, the talk with Rod, had made her much more curious about John than she had been before.

But it was too much for her now. She covered her mother with a blanket, propped John's graduation picture up on top of the television, went into her bedroom and collapsed across her bed.

"Dear Kathy," John's first letters began. "How are you? I am fine . . ." They were the kind of letters a boy might send a girl he had met at camp the summer before. His handwriting was clumsy, and his short messages filled up all the space on the pages. There were also Christmas cards, birthday cards, a huge Valentine with passionate X's and O's. Most of the messages were filled with gossip about friends, private jokes, codelike references to adventures that might or might not have occurred.

Apparently these were the letters Kathy had treasured most. They had more wrinkles and creases than the later ones; they had been filed away in a shoe box in chronological order with tissue paper between each envelope. There were long intervals between the last letters in this series, then a gap where there were no letters at all; the two of them had obviously been close enough during this period to make writing unnecessary. But then something must have happened. When the letters resumed, they were the let's-keep-in-touch kind only one of the two people involved is foolish enough to take seriously. Ordinarily, this would be the end. But in John's case there was another stage, one for which none of his previous letters could have prepared her. After two years' silence, he unexpectedly started writing her again—long, rambling letters written in the climbing, leaping scrawl of his extravagant longhand, five pages, ten pages, twenty. Explanations of some sort, curious autobiographical fragments, they had scarcely a single reference to the girl to whom he was supposedly writing until the very end when a banal message would be tacked on in a P.S. below his name: "Hello to everyone at home for me please. Be a good girl. Cheers, John."

They were soliloquies, not letters. Elaine could understand how embarrassing they must have seemed to Kathy and why, after reading one or two, she didn't want to open the rest. They must have seemed incomprehensible reminders of someone she had long since relegated to her past—something to be returned to his parents, unopened and unread. Elaine herself hesitated for a long time before she opened any more. Once she actually started, though, she double-read each paragraph, becoming so involved that it took her mother's restless pacing across the ceiling to break the spell. Reluctantly, she tucked the letters away in a drawer with the shorter ones he'd sent his parents and went upstairs to fix lunch, wondering about the questions his letters had raised.

Why had he written them? For whom? The Kathy of the early letters was identifiable enough—there were pictures of her among the other past things Mr. Powers had sent down. They showed a tall girl, pretty in a way that could turn out to be either beautiful or arrogant once she got older. Studying the photos of her with John on a ski slope or dressed for a prom, it was easy to imagine people saying what a splendid couple they made. It was only after she removed him from the picture that any strain showed. His head, tilted sideways toward where hers had been, now looked wistful. Her eyes, now that they looked off into a jagged corner, seemed vacant. Elaine would press the two severed halves together, trying to recapture their superficial contentment. But it was too late for that. As puzzled as he looked, John seemed more natural alone. As listless as Kathy's gaze was, it seemed directed to a horizon on which another man would shortly appear.

Ignoring the pictures, concentrating on the letters instead, it was even harder to come up with any relationship that made sense. His stream-of-consciousness, his soul-searching seemed to have little connection with the red-headed, prep-school girl who would clearly never lack for men.

After lunch, Elaine reached into the drawer for his earlier letters, those he had written home from school the year he was fourteen. They weren't as revealing as the ones he'd sent Kathy. No matter how many times Elaine read them, they never became anything but the most commonplace, dutiful notes of a most commonplace, dutiful son. He described different sports in excruciating detail. He remembered to ask how various relatives were. He referred to his mother by her first name. He was vague about his teachers, precise about his friends. He liked folk music and jazz. He went to chapel on Sundays because he enjoyed singing hymns. He was a Red Sox fan. He had fond thoughts about his boat.

The more she studied the family letters, the more ordinary they seemed: I'm okay, food's good, rained yesterday. She began wondering if this wasn't their secret—a commonplaceness so unrelenting that it had to be deliberate. Seen from this angle, they became the letters of a boy who at the age of fourteen had already learned to hide the feelings most important to him. But if this interpretation was true, it led to more questions. What feelings? Why hide them? Was he in awe of his own abilities, unable to reconcile them with the darker emotions anyone has in growing up? Did he instinctively decide his private thoughts were so different from those of his parents that they must be kept temporarily underground?

Elaine had always attached great importance to letters, ever since the time, when she was twelve, that she had accidentally stumbled on those her father had sent her mother during each of his two wars. They were V-mail mostly, the photostat and miniaturization making them seem oddly formal. For reasons best known to her mother, they had been stuffed away inside an old pillowcase with shreds of gift wrapping and tinsel. Elaine used to run back to her room to read them, forgetting her homework in her excitement. She pored over them in the same intense way she now pored over John's, as if by staring hard enough at the page she could shut out the rest of the world and focus past the handwriting to the unknown person behind.

Her father's letters were simple and touching in the way they tried to assure her mother that everything was fine. "Don't sweat about me," he wrote. "This is a picnic compared to what some poor bastards get stuck with. Remember me to Queens!" He had been twenty in 1943. By the time he re-enlisted for Korea, he was almost thirty, but his letters didn't change. ("Greetings from Asia," he'd write. "Merry Christmas from Asia," "Good-by for now from Asia," Asia this, Asia that—the word seemed to hold a special fascination for him, like "abracadabra," the key to unlocking the mysterious wonderland he found himself caught up in. Elaine would lie on her bed and say it out loud, over and over, Asia, Asia, Asia, faster and faster, until it became a nonsense word that made her feel dizzy and she had to stop.) He wrote frequently about Elaine, asking how she was, talking about things they would do together once he got home. "Tell Elaine to practice her roller-skating. Hey, Elaine! Practice your roller-skating, okay, kid? Daddy's going to take you to that rink over in Woodhaven when I get home. You and me are going to show the world what skating's all about!" Elaine read these letters with tears in her eyes, but it wasn't until later that she actually cried.

She brought them downstairs at the end of the week, after not having read them in years. She brought all her mother's and her own past things down, filling up the spaces on the workshop shelves that hadn't been appropriated by the past things Mr. Powers had sent. It occurred to her that if she mended the rips and erased the smudges in their photographs, her mother might take more interest in them, pay less attention to John's letters.

131

But it didn't work out that way. Sunday morning, when Elaine handed her a restored snapshot taken at her high school graduation—Elaine clutching her diploma like a warrant freeing her from prison, Mrs. Collier drunk on faculty champagne—she refused to have anything to do with it. Instead, she went over to the front window and stood staring down at the sidewalk, waiting for the mailman.

"Has it come, my love?"

"Not yet, Mommy."

"But it's not like him to go so long without writing. You don't think something's wrong, do you?"

"Today's Sunday. We don't get mail on Sundays."

This was a mistake. Her mother paced the floor all afternoon, mumbling to herself, frantic in a way she hadn't been all week. Elaine tried putting the television on for her, talking with her, tucking her into bed for a nap, but nothing worked. She refused to be soothed. Finally, with a sleepless night ahead for both of them, Elaine had had no choice.

"Here's one. Are you happy now?"

"But I thought you said there wasn't any mail today."

"It was special delivery. The bell rang while you were watching television."

"Oh."

They had a new routine now. Elaine stopped work when the mailman came. She took her scissors and a pen and met him at the door. When she went upstairs with the letters he had delivered, she added one of John's for her mother to find, hesitating at the head of the stairs only long enough to cut the word "Kathy" off the top and substitute a new salutation in the narrow margin his handwriting had left above the first paragraph. "Dear Mother," she wrote. "Dear Mother and Elaine . . ."

* * *

"Big gray warehouse. Remember it? On the Vineyard near the docks off State Road. The black line they painted at the high-water mark during Hurricane Lucy in the Sky with Diamonds or whatever it was called. That's exactly what they should paint across that entire November if you ask me. One gigantic black stripe. Everything's one way before, everything's another way after. You probably should paint it right across that last week with a circle around the 22nd. The 22nd, three days after the last game I ever played. Last game of anything, not just soccer. Dartmouth, home. No one scored on me all season. We'd go around to all these different campuses and one field would be smoother than the next. Green, not a leaf on them. The John Powers theory of goal-tending made simple: What you do is sweep anything that's not perfectly green from your field of vision. It's very visual, goal-tending. Here comes a leaf, SAVE! Here comes a ball, SAVE!!!

"But it's practically December. The field? Forget it. All covered with dead leaves. Right away I knew I was in trouble. Before the game everyone's pounding me on the back psyching me up. Yeah, John. Yeah, Powers. Know what? I just decided I didn't give a damn any more. One minute I'm Mr. Goalie, screaming at my fullback, hopping up and down to get a better look at the ball, not a second later I'm wondering what in hell am I doing here? I remember because a bird flew by. It caught my eye. I looked up, noticed the Green Mountains off in the distance behind the other goal. Already snow on the tops. I started thinking how nice it would be to be up there hiking. I don't know if you remember seeing this when you came up, but I thought about this saying they had chiseled in marble over the chapel: 'The Strength of the Hills is His Also.' It never occurred to me before that you might need strength from somewhere, especially from mountains. Before that week strength was just something you had. But what I'm trying (not very well) to explain is that was the *first* time I ever took my eye off the field for even a second: 'EYE

ON THE BALL, JOHN! EYE ON THE GODDAMN BALL!,'
which is all I ever heard growing up. The tenth, I mean the
eleventh commandment. But for once in my life I'm watching
this bird. When I turned back to the game, everything had
changed. It was like I had never really seen a soccer field before.
It was beautiful, the fields below the mountains, the coeds standing there with their hands in their coat pockets trying to keep
warm and cheer at the same time, players spreading apart, closing
in, the blue and green shirts, the way the ball sailed against the
sky. I'm standing there lost in it all when I feel something brush
my shoulder. The next thing I know the players in green are
screaming and hugging one another and someone is patting me
on the back to console me. I turn around, and sure enough there's
the ball in the back of the net. I had no idea how it got there.

"Next day was the start of basketball practice. I didn't go.
Didn't go to classes either. Didn't go all week. I don't know what
I expected from my professors. Whatever, I knew I wasn't getting
it any more. No way. So I'd spend most of my time in the library
reading books they never mentioned. It was like I'd just discovered two worlds. One I'd been brought up in and world number
two. Different ideas, different beliefs, different people. Byrne, for
instance. Talk about different. Here I was flying home weekends
to go to coming-out parties for these girls I grew up with (yours
was nice, I'm only kidding). On the way to the airport I'd pass
Byrne standing there on the highway, his thumb stuck out, hitch-
ing up to Montreal for the whores. Albert Phineas Byrne. His
father's in jail for beating up his mom. He was the smartest guy
on campus, but his grades stunk. He told me once all professors
were fools. We used to sit talking in his room. I was his convert.
I didn't dare tell him my old man owned a factory that employed
two thousand people. When he asked me about him, I told him
Dad was a druggist. Big joke, right? I used to go into this long
explanation about how I helped out at the soda fountain when I
was a kid so my mother could go home and fix us dinner. Poor

but proud, the whole routine. Half the people at college were lying about their parents, not just me. Put on old clothes, put on new parents. It was all part of constructing the image you wanted.

"Word got home soon enough. Did you get their version? Dad probably figured I'd gone into shock on account of the goal. They'd been planning to come up for parents' weekend. I guess the dean must have written them about the cuts. They phoned to say they were coming up early. Dad gave me his usual bullshit about canceling these important business appointments for me. Carol kept insisting I was ill. It wasn't until they hung up it occurred to me maybe she was right. I was scared. I'd been scared before without telling anyone, but this was the real thing. See, all along I'd been brought up just like you. Do well in school, do well in sports, go to a good school, and you've got it made. All along it was enough for me, then—forget it. BANG, trajectory ended. POOF. John Powers, spent rocket at eighteen. I lost interest in everything. You know how much I like to eat? Well, it was all I could do to drag myself down to the cafeteria. Starve? Sure, why not. Eat? Well, okay. If somebody feeds me. *That* kind of mood. I finally decided I was in big trouble if I didn't get some help. I called up the infirmary and made an appointment with the college psychiatrist for Friday afternoon. Friday morning I tried going to English class. Halfway there I started thinking about the condescending way this professor talked about Robert Frost. Thought about him, thought about the pimple-faced monstrosity who sat behind me finding phallic symbols in 'Stopping by Woods on a Snowy Evening.' I mean, I was just NOT in the mood. What I did instead was walk out of town until the houses ended and I could see out across the apple orchards to the Adirondacks. An incredible day for that time of year, too. Sunny. Warm. It could have been September.

"They were waiting for me when I got back. Dad still had his business suit on like he'd run out of a conference halfway through. Carol was all dressed up, which kind of bothered me. Dad treats her like a Barbie doll half the time. She looks really great when she's wearing old clothes and baggy sweaters, things like that. Really *comfortable*. But Dad gets all upset if she isn't dressed like Elizabeth Taylor. He's always buying her new clothes, and Carol puts them on just to keep him happy. But anyway, she came right over and kissed me. The moment she let go Dad started in with that take-charge way of his. What's wrong, son? What happened? HOW MUCH WILL IT COST??? Driving up there they must have decided I'd flipped out altogether. I guess they were surprised I sounded normal. Dad wanted something dramatic he could throw his weight against. When I told him about the psychiatrist, it was like puncturing a balloon. The appointment wasn't until five. We had the whole afternoon to kill. When they saw I wasn't foaming at the mouth or anything, they decided to change tactics, pretend everything was fine. Carol asked me if there were any nice rides we could take. Dad let me drive. I took them out the same way I walked, only farther, all the way to Lake Champlain. It wasn't frozen yet. It was so blue it hurt your eyes. Across the bridge in New York is a park at Crown Point (it's probably a drive-in movie by now, but it was nice then). I remembered reading about the fort they used to have there in those Kenneth Roberts books I loved as a kid. I must have read *Northwest Passage* twenty-eight times. So we decided to stop. It's not restored or anything. There are these old walls you can walk to but that's about all. Carol, I suppose by prearrangement, stayed behind in the car.

"It was the facts of life all over again. We found a bench we could sit on. Right away he started with his football-coach lecture about discipline and pride. I was ruining my chance in life. I was wasting myself. I was, horror upon horror, LETTING THEM DOWN!!! Any moment I expected him to say 'Eye on the ball, John. Eye on the goddamn ball.' But I listened for a while without saying anything. I then made the mistake of mentioning Byrne. That was good for five minutes' worth on 1) lazy beatniks ruining the country; 2) irresponsible radicals getting the blacks all riled up; 3) Byrne probably teaching me how to smoke dope. But it didn't bother me as much as you might think. There's a secret about Dad no one knows. This typical Wasp, conservative, bigoted view of the world isn't really him at all. He's too damn shrewd for that. He puts it on and takes it off, the same way these bleeding-heart liberals do when they pretend to turn themselves into vegetarians for peace on earth goodwill toward men. But give Dad credit. At least he still has a sense of humor about it. I'll say something like, 'Come on, Dad. You don't really mean that. Send them all to Russia? Every last one? Even the babies, Dad?' and I'll laugh and he'll laugh, too, despite himself. But here's the thing. I'm the only one, the ONLY one, take my word for it, who knows how to shake him out of it. Without me all the conservative bullshit will become the real him after a while. A suit he's worn so often he can't take it off.

"This time I just waited it out. We walked down to the beach through an old tunnel. Except for that and a few openings for cannon to poke through there wasn't much left. Later on a ranger gave us a brochure saying how they were going to restore the fort eventually. I thought it was fine just the way it was. Dad had trouble with the rocks getting down there. The lake must have dropped recently because there was a lot of sand and pebbles you could walk along without getting your feet wet. A lot of driftwood, too. I picked up a piece to take back to Carol, then I found a better one a few yards away. Next to it was the skeleton of a dead seagull. It was bleached white from the sun. There were little tufts of feather still attached to the bone.

"I guess the atmosphere finally got to me. For the first time that week, I felt really good. Content. Strong in a way I never had been before. Off to the right is this statue of Champlain standing up in a canoe with some Indians looking down the lake he discovered. He's shielding his eyes with his hand. Ahead of us was his lake. It looks exactly like it must have when he first saw it. Blue.

Unspoiled. Behind us was the fort. This crumbling fort hidden in vines. All this beauty and promise spread out in front of us so close it seemed you could reach out and take it in your hands. It was like staring at all the fantasies I had when I was a kid about the French and Indian Wars, Robert Rogers, the Revolution, Ethan Allen, all that. All the promise that was there, not the Pledge of Allegiance bullshit, not the Fourth of July or the flag. The idea of it. The potential. I never felt so close to it before. Vermont, Lake Champlain, the Adirondacks. But it wasn't just what was there in front of us, because it was so clear that last day I felt we were sitting on a mountain top where we could see over the horizon toward the Great Lakes and the Plains, all in the same glance. See down toward Virginia, out past the Gulf States into Texas. Out across the Rockies to California. And no matter which way we looked, east, west, north, south, everywhere was just as blue and calm and perfect as right there on the summit. As if no one had ever seen it before or messed it up. Pioneers, cowboys, miners, we had beat all of them to it, just like old Champlain there, turned into bronze the moment he discovered it.

" 'I think we better get back to Carol,' Dad said. He tossed a pebble at Champlain. 'She'll think we drowned.'

"His voice broke the mood. I still don't know what caused it. I suppose I was at the point where I needed something bigger than better grades and scoring more baskets, and America was it. If we had gone to a cathedral that day instead of Crown Point, I probably would have ended up wanting to be a monk.

"It was still too early to go back to town. Fort Ticonderoga wasn't far. We decided to drive down there. It was just about the only place we'd missed when I was a kid. By the time we arrived it was cloudy out. The gates were open, but because it was late in the season there were only a few tourists inside. They had some men dressed like Colonial soldiers. People were taking their picture. I didn't enjoy it as much as Crown Point. The lake didn't seem as pretty without the sun. There was a pulp mill in town.

The air smelled like tear gas, and it was all you could do to breathe. If I remember right, Carol even covered her nose with a handkerchief. We were standing there on one of the ramparts pretending to enjoy ourselves when one of the guides came over with a transistor radio looped around his musket. He had a funny expression on his face. 'They just shot the President,' he said with a little grin.

"Like everyone else we ran back to our car for the radio. As we drove over to Vermont, they announced he was dead, but the static was so bad Carol finally shut it off. I don't think the significance had sunk in yet. There was still my psychiatrist appointment. It never occurred to us not to go. Dad parked in front of my dorm to unload a few things they had brought along to make me feel more at home. A tennis racket, a lamp. In the back of the trunk was my old football. Before I could stop her, Carol took it out. 'Go out for a pass!' she yelled.

"I never saw her do anything like that before. Feeling jerky, I trotted out over the lawn. Sure enough, she threw it to me. Clumsily, like a girl. I picked it up and started walking back to the car, but then Dad started running, too, waving his arm. I fired it as hard as I could, hitting him in the chest above the heart, almost knocking him down. 'Hey, *nice* toss, John. Your turn, Carol. Heads up!'

"It was starting to rain. Kennedy had just been shot by a man whose name we didn't know. My mother and father were running across a wet lawn trying to make me feel better by playing catch. My mother's hands are so small, she kept dropping the ball each time she tried to throw it. My father kept losing sight of it in the mist. For a reason I'm not sure of, I suddenly felt an overwhelming pity for them that was stronger than anything I've ever known. I didn't want Carol to grow old. I didn't want Dad to get intolerant and hard. I didn't want the world to change. I wanted everything to stay exactly the way it was. But because they're my parents, because the comforting had always been the other way around, I couldn't go over and tell them how sorry I was about disappointing them. I couldn't take them in my arms, tell them somehow everything will be fine. In the rain, in the dark, the only thing I could do to comfort them was to arc the ball higher and softer, making it easier for them to catch . . ."

It didn't take Elaine long to read the letter. Despite the differences in their upbringings, she found herself nodding in recognition at the things he had to say. Like John, she remembered the confidence of her generation in the early sixties, the feeling that she was on a mountain top with the future at her feet. Like John, she remembered the vision being suddenly spoiled, though it would never have occurred to her to talk of her disillusionment in terms of America as John did. The autumn of 1963 was, to her, the autumn she had won the scholarship to college; the day Kennedy had been shot was, to her, the day her mother started talking out loud to Mildred Sayers, dead thirty years. John had the knack of linking his personal concerns to events in the larger world, whereas Elaine had always done just the opposite—ignored the world in her absorption with her problems at home. But John's letter made it seem as though he had witnessed that crucial November for her and was writing to explain. Cutting out Kathy's name and putting her own in its place had been simple, but it was John—in the vividness of his description, in his effort to relate his feelings at an age and in a year she had shared—who had completed the process, making the letter seem really hers after all.

Every Sunday her mother demanded more of him. She waved her wrist proudly toward the screen each time he appeared, commenting on how his blond hair was like her father's, insisting Elaine run the film through again until she agreed on the resemblance. Every Wednesday, the mailman arrived with another package of past things Mr. Powers wanted erased, college things now—souvenir mugs, yearbooks, a few faded snapshots dimmer than the earlier ones, as if matching John's new lack of focus with their own. Every Thursday, Mrs. Powers phoned to thank her for neatening up what few odds and ends the two of them had managed to save over the years. "You're so *good* with them," she said. "You're just like one of Santa's little elves."

Every Friday, Elaine was in despair, wondering how much longer she could keep it up. The splices were becoming too difficult, the gaps in their lives all but impossible to reconcile. At thirteen she had already gone to work part-time at a stationery store up the street. At thirteen John was already at prep school; pictures of him dressed in choir robes beside the chapel clashed ludicrously with pictures of her dressed in carbon-stained smocks by the cash register. At fourteen he was restless; pictures showed him scowling, standing by a trout stream with his rod dipped toward the water, indifferent as to whether he caught any fish or not. At fourteen she was dishing out gravy in a run-down cafeteria after school, too busy to be anything. She pasted the photo of him fishing on a scrapbook page next to one of her teetering along the edge of a dirty pond in Forest Park on a rare day off. It became harder and harder to link six-year-old John on pony-back with six-year-old Elaine on various chipped and rusting merry-go-rounds, glossy color portraits of him with grimy black-and-whites she and her friends had made in bus stations. But somehow, remembering her own empty nightmares, remembering the way her mother had been before John, she always managed to combine them in time for Sunday. John and Elaine riding mechanical horses at Coney Island—Elaine sitting comfortably in jeans, gesturing backward to reassure John who looked out of place in riding-school jodphurs. John and Elaine wedged against each other in a cold, do-it-yourself photo booth beneath Jamaica Station—the rich boy transposed to working-class Queens.

The other past things were even harder to merge. By December her mother had improved to the point where Elaine decided to risk buying a Christmas tree, their first in ten years. When it came time to decorate it, she found that the ornaments that had survived the fire were too few to cover more than two or three branches near the bottom. She filled in the rest with decorations that had belonged to John: huge, satin-covered balls that completely dwarfed the tin Santas and plastic angels her father had once bought for her. When she was finished, it seemed more allegory than Christmas tree, a procession upward from the broken, make-do world of their own past to the glittering, ostentatious display of the Powers.

She had lunch with Mr. Powers that week, the first time she had seen him since the summer. They had planned to get together in the fall, but Mr. Powers had called at the last moment to say he was ill, promising her they would make a date for the following week instead. The following week, Mrs. Powers, who was much improved, had "commandeered" him to man a booth at their church's holiday fair.

"I'm sorry," he said over the phone. "I hope this won't make a difference."

"A difference in what?"

"Things are still going well with the work, aren't they? You're not running out of steam or anything, I hope."

"I'm still working on John if that's what you mean. How much longer I'll be able to is another question."

She was about to tell him that she needed more past things—the rest of John's letters, any stray photographs Mrs. Powers may have hidden. But before she could start, he abruptly cut her off.

"I'd rather not talk business right now," he said. "I called to find out if you'd be interested in going into the city with me on Sunday. We could watch the skaters and grab some lunch."

"I thought you said you were busy?"

"I'll duck out early. I really would like to see you, Elaine. I know how depressing it must be for you not having anywhere to go this time of year. . . . Shall I pick you up around twelve?"

Elaine put the phone down, wondering why the prospect of seeing him left her feeling so indifferent. His call had irritated her—she had been going through some of the Christmas gifts John had received in college and she had resented the interruption. Then, too, Mr. Powers had been so ready to take what she said as a complaint, so anxious to sweep it aside by asking her out when only a minute before he'd insisted he was busy.

She was still wondering about this when Sunday came. For a while she had considered calling him back, breaking their date just to see what his reaction would be. She finally decided not to; she wanted to test her own feelings, not just his, and it would be a better test in person.

"Merry Christmas!" Mr. Powers said when she answered the door. He had a big smile on his face, and he handed her a gift-wrapped package.

"For your mother," he explained. "I hope she likes eggnog. How is she?"

"Very good lately. How's Carol?"

"Terrific!" He helped her on with her coat. "All set for a nice afternoon? I hope you don't mind my singing, because I intend to try out every carol in my repertoire. Any requests?"

He sang with the radio all the way to Manhattan, switching from station to station until he found a song he liked. They parked in a garage on Thirty-fourth Street and walked up Fifth Avenue toward the park, window-shopping, stopping to listen to madrigal singers on the steps of St. Patrick's, then going to the café next to the skating rink where they could sit and talk out of the cold.

"I've never seen you in a better mood," she said when they had sat down. "Is it Christmas?"

"Partly. I'm really in the spirit for a change. It doesn't seem as sad as it usually does. I haven't felt this way in years, not since . . . Carol got sick."

"You were going to say since John died."

"Was I?" he said vaguely. "Listen, there are still about a dozen carols I haven't subjected you to yet, and unless you promise to relax and enjoy yourself I'm going to start singing them here and now."

He reached into his jacket pocket for his wallet. "Speaking of Christmas, have I ever shown you this?"

For a moment she thought it was a picture of him with John, the two of them with their arms around each other's shoulders in front of a Christmas tree. But the willing, enthusiastic closeness of the pose meant it couldn't be John. When she examined it more carefully, she saw that the boy she had thought was John was dressed in the kind of corduroy knickers that had been popular in the thirties; that the man had a much sharper profile than Mr. Powers and wasn't quite as tall.

"My father," Mr. Powers explained. "That was taken the year I was thirteen. I remember we had Christmas dinner at the country club that year and came back home to open the gifts. It was midnight before we were done . . . I know this sounds pompous, but my father was the greatest man I have ever known."

"He looks awfully dignified," Elaine said.

"He was, at least on the surface. He was brought up in the old school. Work hard, respect your elders, go to church on Sundays. He even wore a pocket watch, a great big silver one. I guess at that age I thought it was all kind of silly. I went through a time in college when I rebelled just like. . . . Everybody goes through a stage when they're ashamed of their parents. Mine didn't last very long, thank God. I got it out of my system. My father and I had talks about all kinds of things. Any problem I had, I could go to him, and he'd listen. I was *proud* of him, not ashamed. I'd come home from college before Christmas, and he'd take me out to lunch at his club, just the two of us, and I'd feel like the luckiest man in the world. . . . It was pretty rough on me when he died. If it hadn't been for meeting Carol, I don't think I would have gotten through it."

"You've never mentioned him before."

"Well, it's not because I don't think about him. There's a picture in my office that's a lot better than this one. His father, my grandfather, is the one who started the company. Started it from nothing, a little shed where he forged propellers for the ferries crossing the Sound. He built it into a million-dollar operation, and Dad took it from there. I stepped in when I got out of the Navy. The three of us were an unbroken chain going all the way back to the 1870's. It could have gone on a lot longer, too. . . ." He broke off abruptly and for no reason at all began to berate the busboy who was taking away their empty coffee cups.

"The picture's falling apart," Elaine said, trying to distract him. "If you like, I can take it home and fix it up. Get rid of the creases and all. If you're not careful, there won't be anything left of it before long."

"No, that's all right," Mr. Powers said quickly. "I know how busy you are."

"I'd be glad to. It won't take very long."

"You won't . . . you won't erase it, will you?"

He made it into a joke, but Elaine could tell he was serious.

"I'm only trying to help."

He didn't answer. He had taken the picture back and was staring at it. Without a word, he put it back in his wallet, the wallet back in his jacket pocket. It was as if the entire conversation had never taken place.

"Had enough?" he asked. "I feel like some fresh air."

"I'd like to stay here."

Mr. Powers had already got up. "Let me help you on with your coat."

"I'd like to stay here," she repeated.

"Why?"

"I want to talk to you."

He let her coat drop over the back of the empty chair and stood watching the skaters. "That sounds ominous," he said without turning his head. "About what?"

"About John."

He looked at her curiously and sat down. He called the waiter over and ordered more coffee.

Elaine could tell he was worried. He drummed his fingers on the table, looking at her in the same calculating way she had seen him look at the businessmen the afternoon of their first lunch. Each time she had seen him, he had given a bit more of himself away; each time, just when she thought he might be ready to lower the barriers, he had slipped back into disguise. She remembered what John had said in the letter about his putting on a role so often he soon wouldn't be able to take it off.

"So," he said once the waiter had gone, "talk away."

"I'm not sure how much longer I can keep working on him," she said carefully, studying his face for his reaction. "I have other projects I've been putting off all fall."

"That's a shame," Mr. Powers said calmly, meeting her eyes. "We're so close to finishing, too. In fact, I think Carol would have forgotten him by now if it weren't for the other things."

It was Elaine's turn to act surprised. "What other things?" she asked.

"Clothes and records and so on. I was going to give them to some charity, but Carol still looks in his closet occasionally. If I could tell her you were patching them up . . ."

"I don't usually patch up clothes," Elaine said quickly, trying to hide her interest. "I have a woman in the Bronx who mends them for me."

"Would you mind if I sent them down? I'm sure it would speed up the process immensely. There's been a big improvement these last few months. She's on the verge of forgetting him completely now. If we can keep it up just a little longer . . ."

Elaine stared out at the skaters, scarcely conscious of what he was saying. There was a little girl by herself near the rail. She fell, pushed herself back up, then fell again. Nobody paid any attention to her; she started to cry.

Elaine turned around.

"What if I say no?"

"Sorry?"

"What if I say no?"

For a moment, Elaine thought he was going to hit her. Every muscle on his face tightened, his hands involuntarily clenched. She was fascinated more than scared—it was like seeing a totally different person.

He didn't hit her. Instead, he leaned toward her until their foreheads were almost touching, traversing in those few seconds all the facial expressions that exist between great anger and calm. When he started talking again, it was in an urgent, confessional whisper that was new to her; she wondered if he held it in reserve for special crises.

"Once Carol's forgotten him we could spend more time together. We wouldn't have the job hanging over us any more . . . I don't think it's any secret that I'm attracted to you, Elaine. The only thing that prevents me from . . ."

"Answer me, Richard! What if I say no?"

"We could plan on seeing a play," he said, talking faster. "We could have dinner somewhere very special."

"Dinner's not enough."

"We could take a drive up along the Hudson some afternoon. There's a winery up there we could see. Didn't you once tell me how much you liked the country? I'm sure of it, Elaine. Remember? It was that time I took you out to lunch. We could take a drive and . . ."

"It's not enough," she said, closing her eyes.

"We could go back out to the Vineyard. We could go back out there and start from where we left off. Just the two of us this time. We could turn off the telephone, build a fire. There are lots of nice walks we could take. Just the two of us, Elaine. Just as soon as she forgets him once and for all."

Every instinct she had was to get up and leave. She could

picture it quite clearly: the look of contempt she would give him as she got up; his bewildered, angry expression of surprise as she buttoned her coat; the purposeful way she would walk past the other tables to the door. She had considered all these stages in her exit, had actually started to push her chair back, when just in time she remembered John.

He was everything now. If she wasn't careful she would spoil it, cut herself off from the rest of his things just when she needed them most. She forced herself to sit still. She smiled at what he said, pretending to be pleased.

"Yes," she said. "Yes, I'd like that, Richard. We could go in the spring once I'm done."

Mr. Powers let his shoulders drop the same way he had the night on Martha's Vineyard when she had refused his offer of a drink. "That's fine, Elaine. I'm really looking forward to it . . . Now how about that fresh air? Shall we walk up to the Guggenheim?"

Halfway to the door, he stopped and hurried back to their table. Elaine saw him talking to the waiter—the waiter was shaking his head. Mr. Powers handed him something, then handed him something else. When he rejoined her, he was holding a menu.

"A souvenir of our afternoon together," he said, leaning over to kiss her.

"Thank you, Richard. That's very sweet."

They didn't get very far uptown. After a few blocks, Elaine complained of a headache and asked him to take her home. They drove back to Queens in silence. Mr. Powers turned the radio on, but the carols seemed to irritate him, and he quickly shut it off. All Elaine could think about was John.

She would have more of him soon. More of him for herself, more of him for her mother. Before, she had always found pleasure in studying John's face because it reminded her of his father's, but now, when she glanced at Mr. Powers behind the wheel, she could see only reminders of John—John's forehead, John's face and eyes.

"Happy?" Mr. Powers asked when he caught her watching him.

"Very happy."

They said good-by at the door. Elaine still had the menu in her hand. The moment he drove away she ripped it in half and dropped it in the garbage with the rest of the day's trash.

After breakfast the next morning, she went down to her workshop and took two more scrapbooks down from the shelves—one of John in the years before he went to college, the other of herself as a girl. John's scrapbooks were so crowded and hers were so empty, it was impossible to combine hers with his instead of the other way around, no matter how much better the pictures might look on the heavier paper with the leather binding. Elaine ran a sharp knife underneath the corners to pry him loose, trimming him out of the larger pictures, spreading paste over the back of him before pressing him firmly down on the flimsy pages inside the cardboard covers. Beside her now in all the pictures was the young boy of the films. The way they dressed still didn't quite match, but it got better the older they became. John was caught up in the casual, dressed-down style his classmates affected their senior year; Elaine, reaching high school, was able to afford nicer clothes.

She could see the changes herself. Pictures that once showed Elaine sitting in a park somewhere, obviously lonely, oddly defiant, turned into souvenirs of a happier Elaine who had been there all along, needing someone sitting next to her to draw out her stifled exuberance, someone to tease her out of her protective shell, to draw away part of the camera's harsh attention onto himself. In the same way, the restlessness—the *apartness*—that had always marked John seemed to be fading, too, to be transformed into concern, an anxious desire to make Elaine sit close enough to him so that the lens captured them both.

It became easier still once they both went away to college. They had gone the same year, might actually have passed each other during one of John's frequent visits to Boston, might conceivably have had mutual friends. For a time their separate worlds had merged; it was simply a matter of linking pictures of her on the Common with pictures of him on the Esplanade until they walked arm-in-arm in an indefinite, springlike park, her calmness and imagination complementing his intensity and strength.

Studying the finished pictures reminded her of the delight she had experienced her freshman year upon finding herself among people her own age who didn't laugh at her because she liked music and books, didn't make fun of her ambition to go into business for herself. It was as if their generation had been deliberately kept apart in small towns across the country until that very moment—the early fall of 1963—when they had finally been allowed to find one another, meld their separate experiences into one, enjoy a golden few years together without a thought of the outside world.

They read the same books now. John's copy of *The Lord of the Rings* was crumpled from a dozen readings; the same passages she had liked were heavily underlined in green. There were ticket stubs from concerts by the same folk groups she had followed, tee-shirts with the familiar slogans pressed across the fronts, ski patches from Vermont mountains near his campus where she had gone on weekend trips her second winter at school. For the first time there were newspaper pictures of her to compare with the ones his mother had saved. Campus newspapers at first, with smudgy, misaligned mentions of scholarships she had recently won. But there were longer articles as well, and Boston papers with stories about the various restoration projects her department was involved in, pictures that showed her standing next to the department chairman inspecting a Federal vase from the Atheneum that was badly in need of repair.

As the years went by, the newspapers changed. The pages didn't rip as easily as those from the fifties. She didn't know whether to attribute this to improved printing techniques or to the bad news that was starting to dominate them—the bold print and screaming captions seemed to give the papers a tensile strength the earlier editions didn't have. Hurricanes that ten years before had moved safely out to sea were now approaching shore. A burning city that in 1956 would have been Budapest or Caracas now turned out to be Detroit.

But the biggest change was in the pictures. There were no more individual shots of John leaping with arms outstretched toward a basket, no more mementos of John accepting another award. There didn't seem to be individual photographs of anyone now. More and more the pages seemed given over to pictures of crowds. Why had Mrs. Powers even bothered saving these editions? Elaine would take out a magnifying glass and go over each picture in turn, holding the page up to the light to see better, folding it back and forth to try to isolate John from the surrounding blur. But no matter how hard she looked, no matter how many concerts and rallies and riots she skimmed through, the faces always refused to separate themselves out into identifiable persons.

There was one picture that especially haunted her, a picture of a civil rights demonstration in the South. It showed dogs straining at their leashes, a church steeple, policemen with bull horns and cattle prods and the familiar, indistinguishable blend of crowd that never varied, as though the same studio extras were transported from picture to picture. In the center was a heavy black woman shielding a little girl with her body, the child prone on the pavement beneath her. Not much of the woman's face was visible: an improbably small nose, one frightened eye, the other covered with blood from a gash on her forehead. But hidden as the face was, it seemed out of all the pictures Elaine had gone through the only one capable of standing alone, and in a queer way it seemed to have some connection with John. The picture of the black woman was somehow just as relevant to her understanding of him as the snapshot that had showed him standing on the diving board on Martha's Vineyard.

Later that afternoon she put the scrapbooks aside and went back to the pile of newspapers until she found the picture again. She spread the page open across the table, weighting the corners to hold it smooth. The woman's picture was near the top of the page. She brought the razor along the right-hand margin and veered in, trimming carefully until the severed picture dropped free. The older newspapers were still in the crate by the file cabinet. She pulled out one at random and leafed through it until she found a picture the same size: children hunting Easter eggs on the White House lawn, April 1959. She fit it into the empty space like a part from a jigsaw puzzle, taped it and held it up to examine the difference the substitution had made. The shot of the rolling lawn seemed to tranquilize the entire page.

She became increasingly involved with the newspapers once Christmas was over. The more she read them, the more they seemed to be installments of a frustratingly complex mystery whose solution was beyond her. She justified the time she spent on them by telling herself it was her own past she was catching up on, not just John's. But if she was honest about it, if she examined her motives, she knew that the real reason was to fill in the gaps caused by the gradual dearth of his pictures.

The permanent cameraman who had seemed to be with the Powers at all times when John was a boy did not accompany him to college. The school blazers, the tuxedos and madras jackets in which he had once posed were also gone. By his last semester in college, the occasional snapshots showed him wearing baggy work pants and nylon windbreakers, reminding Elaine not of the trendy, deliberately scruffy men she had known in college, who had favored army jackets and faded jeans, but of boys her age in high school who had dropped out before graduation to work in factories or garages.

The last home movie in which John appeared was taken at a cousin's wedding in the early fall of 1966. He appeared twice, the first time incidentally, standing near the bride and groom's limousine. Just before the film ended, he appeared again. The camera had been focusing on Mr. and Mrs. Powers, standing by themselves on the porch of what looked like a country club. Mr. Powers was smiling his best politician's smile, gesturing to someone out of sight on the left. It was John. The camera moved in that direction just long enough to catch him turning away from his parents, walking down the flagstone steps that led to the driveway. When the camera returned to Mr. and Mrs. Powers, Mr. Powers was staring after him in bewilderment. His smile was gone now. He let his outstretched arm fall slowly to his side in a pathetic gesture of regret. Elaine ran the film back a dozen times, slowing it down, trying to read what was on John's face, missing it in the shadows cast by a striped tent, then picking up Mr. Powers again calling to his son, reaching for him, watching him go.

"We had an argument at the reception," Mr. Powers explained when he called to wish her a happy New Year and she asked him about it. "He was into this fantasy about quitting college before the end of the year and going off on his own to see the country. I suppose I lost my temper. I called him a gutless hippy, that kind of thing. I wish to hell he had been a hippy. That kind of rebellion would have been kid's stuff compared to what happened. It was the last time we ever saw him."

"Don't bother sending the film back. In fact you can burn it for all I care. I'll be sending you down his clothes tomorrow. You can burn those, too. Carol doesn't even look at them any more."

After he hung up, she went over to her desk for John's last picture. As it turned out, it was the easiest of all. It meshed perfectly with the single college snapshot she had saved of herself, requiring no trimming whatever: John standing alone on a snowy street in Vermont turned into John standing beside her near Harvard Square, their shoulders leaning against each other for support, their faces turned defiantly toward the lens as if together they could conquer the world.

She didn't put this picture away in the scrapbook with the others. She found a little frame for it and set in on her dresser. It was the last thing she saw when she went to bed at night, the first thing she saw on waking. Sometimes she actually dreamed of him standing beside her, listening sympathetically to her problems, cheering her up with some silly joke only the two of them understood, asking her for advice in turn. When she woke up, she was still talking to him; she would listen to the half of herself that was dreaming out loud with the half of herself that was already awake, illusion and reality battling, illusion temporarily winning, making her feel warm and content. But then her mother's alarm clock would go off in the next room, and the vision she had of him disappeared, faded into the chronic white gaps of her nightmares, his hands disappearing last of all, as though he were being swallowed up in quicksand.

"Good-by, John," she would mumble in the dream, not quite ready to give him up. "Take care of yourself, okay? Okay, John? Okay?"

It was hard for Elaine to give up John for even a little while, and she resented the other jobs that still demanded her attention. Other people's past things seemed boring and irrelevant compared to his; she found it difficult to summon up enough enthusiasm to make even the smallest repairs. But she forced herself to make them now. By clearing her desk of all those projects, she could afford to devote a month or two to John alone.

Most of the work didn't take very long. There were the usual films and scrapbooks, a few paintings, nothing special. She worked every day for a week, and then there was only one project left that wasn't somehow connected to John: Olga's piece of fabric.

She felt guilty about it. Despite her promise to Olga, she hadn't worked on it; her efforts had consisted mainly of taking it out of the cabinet, staring at it, shaking her head and putting it back again. She decided she had procrastinated long enough. There had never been a past thing she couldn't fix, and she would fix this one, even if she needed somebody else's help.

She would take it to Juanita.

In some respects, Juanita was a past thing herself, a link to the girl Elaine had once been. They had worked in the cafeteria together when they were in high school, Juanita ladling gravy over the potatoes Elaine dished out. Juanita could hardly speak English in those days, but it wasn't long before they discovered the great secret that they shared: they were both ambitious, Elaine to go to college, Juanita to become a seamstress with her own shop.

They had kept in touch over the years. Juanita had opened her shop in the Bronx at about the same time that Elaine started her business, and Elaine soon got into the habit of taking her clients' old wedding dresses up there. Elaine herself wasn't very good at mending them. No matter how long she hung the patches of fabric outside in the sun to fade, no matter how many old clothing stores she went through to find a matching material, she had never been able to duplicate the soft, fragile patina of age the dress had taken on. Juanita's talent was that she had discovered a way to take patches off the dress itself, like a doctor replacing scarred facial tissue with a graft from his patient's thigh.

"As good as old," Elaine would say when she picked the dress up. Juanita and her sewing girls would laugh at this. Juanita would take the dress in her arms, reluctant to let it go, and press her cheeks against the fabric as if she herself were the bride.

"Why you make it so difficult on me?" she'd say, peeking coyly up at Elaine from behind one fold. "Such a pretty woman to be always with something old."

It was hard to imagine two things more different than a wedding dress and Olga's fabric, but Elaine decided the principle was the same. She would take it to Juanita, let Juanita match it from her huge stock of material and bring the new fabric to Olga so she could make her own repairs. Once that was done, her conscience would be clear—she would be left with only John.

The shop had changed since the last time Elaine was there. The front was now a display window with bridal mannequins spinning clockwise on mechanical turntables, their peach-colored arms held sideways, palms up, in the condescending gesture of queens acknowledging their court's adoration. "Dreamland Wedding Boutique," flashed the new neon sign in English, then in Spanish. Chimes went off as Elaine opened the door. What had once been a workroom littered with fabric was now a showroom lined with mirrors; the sewing machines had been banished to a loft down the street. A young woman in a white blazer took Elaine's name. There was no sign of the sewing girls she had once loved to tease.

Even Juanita herself had changed. She greeted Elaine as warmly as ever, but she seemed fleshier, and she had the apologetic air of someone who has struck it rich and can't quite believe it.

"People all the time want to get married," she explained when Elaine congratulated her. "We tell them, '*Señorita,* we will make you into a princess for one day. A princess, *señorita!* Guaranteed!' "

She ran down the list of sewing girls Elaine remembered. Carla had quit to be married; Juanita had given her a dress. Maria Sanchez had quit to be married; Juanita had given her a dress. Tina Cabrillo was engaged and had given notice; Juanita had *promised* her a dress, but only if she swore to name her first daughter "Juanita."

"And you, Elaine? I will make you into a princess someday, *también,* and then I will retire to San Juan and live happy ever afterward."

"You will be a very old woman when that happens, Juanita. But weddings aren't why I've come. Is there somewhere we can talk?"

Juanita led her past the fitting rooms to a little office. There was a sewing machine against one wall and an old metal file cabinet overflowing with patterns. Juanita poured Elaine some coffee. In this setting she seemed more like the Juanita Elaine remembered.

"Did you bring me something old, Elaine? Something old I fix new, only old?"

" 'As good as old,' as I used to say."

"*Sí.* As good as old."

Elaine opened her pocketbook. "I wouldn't bother you with this, except it's for a friend of mine."

She put the fabric on the card table Juanita used as her desk. Juanita frowned. She made no move to pick it up.

"I don't want you to sew anything this time," Elaine said quickly. "I just want you to find some fabric that matches it."

"For what, Elaine? For a shroud?"

"I know it's ugly. It's supposed to be ugly. It's a uniform, the kind they used to wear in the camps."

"Like that man's you once brought me at Easter? The man who had the sweater the moths ate?"

Elaine shook her head. "No, that was *summer* camp, Juanita. This is a concentration camp I'm talking about. In the war. Olga wasn't Jewish, but they took her family there anyway."

"What war?"

"World War II. They must have taught you about it in school. They brought people on cattle trains to these camps and put them in ovens."

Juanita got up from her chair and walked over to the sewing machine. She stared at Elaine as she described the camps, pursing her lips and giving a little shiver of disgust when she looked at the patch of cloth.

"I never heard of that," she said, shaking her head emphatically. "In school we learned sewing and cooking. No wars. We were too busy for wars."

"Millions of people died, Juanita. Olga was one of the few who didn't. This is part of the uniform she wore all the time. She wants to fix it up so she can remember what her life was like before."

"Before what?"

"Before . . . Listen, all I want you to do is match it. I'd do it myself if I had the time to go searching around. It *has* to be matched, Juanita. There must be a special kind of burlap or something."

Juanita laughed. "There is nothing so ugly in the entire world. I think you should forget about wars and camps. That was all a long time ago. You go home and bring me a nice wedding dress like you used to. I fix it up myself. I take it and find a way to patch it up like in the good old days. Okay, Elaine? You come back tomorrow and we have a nice long talk about Columbus and the Pledge of Allegiance and all the nice history you want."

"Juanita!"

Juanita got up, pushed back the curtain that separated her office from the fitting rooms and yelled something in Spanish to the girl in the blazer.

"I have to go now, Elaine. You come back tomorrow when you are feeling better. I will show you the dress I am making Tina."

Elaine put the piece of fabric back in her pocketbook. Juanita walked her to the door.

"I tell you what," she said as Elaine was about to leave. "I can't help you, but you try Mario's. Do you know Mario's? There is everything there in the way of old clothes. If you can't find your material there, you can't find it anywhere."

She gave Elaine the address. But Elaine didn't go there right away, even though it was on the next block. She wanted to collect her thoughts first. She found a coffee shop across the street and sat there nursing a cup of tea for so long the waitress came over and asked if anything was wrong.

"No. No, I'm fine," Elaine said, a bit too loudly. A man in a lumberjack shirt swiveled around on his stool to stare at her; another man whispered something in his ear, and they both laughed. As she went to pay her check she caught sight of herself in the mirror behind the take-out counter and understood why. She saw the unkempt hair, the ancient gray topcoat she had grabbed from her mother's closet that morning without thinking, the lines under her eyes that she no longer bothered to smooth away, and it seemed to her to be someone else's pathetic reflection—a shopping-bag lady who had somehow snuck up behind her when she wasn't looking, killing time in the coffee shop just as Elaine was, needing someone to share her memories with, reminiscing to the teacup for lack of anyone human.

"What am I turning into?" she wondered, making a futile effort to pat her hair into place. She hurried outside without waiting for her change.

She tried to flag a cab, then thought better of it and started to walk to the bus stop. On the way she passed a small dress shop.

Ordinarily, she was careful about buying new clothes, but this was an emergency. She went in. There was a navy-blue skirt her size on sale at half-price. She found a peach-colored top to go with it and was reaching into her pocketbook to pay for them when her hand brushed against Olga's fabric.

"Could you send them?" she asked, thrusting the money at the saleswoman. "I still have one or two errands to do."

The dress shop was at the end of a long block of specialty stores and boutiques that included Juanita's. The next block was much shorter; it branched diagonally to the right and ended at a municipal garage. Elaine walked past an abandoned hot-dog stand, an army-and-navy store that had a steel grill over its window, and two small tailoring shops, neither of which she had the nerve to enter alone. Mario's, when she finally found it, turned out to be behind the bus garage, standing alone on a block of recently demolished tenements. There was a Nehi ad from the thirties splashed across one brick wall. The adjacent buildings had been torn down to reveal the old-fashioned bottle and the faded red and black lettering across its throat.

"Help you, lady?" a nervous little man asked the moment she walked in.

"I'm just browsing, thank you."

The man climbed back on his stool. "Browse your life away, lady," he mumbled.

It was dark in the shop after the street. Elaine stumbled toward the back, feeling as though she had entered a cave. The first thing she was able to distinguish in the gloom was a row of metal bins filled with old clothing—shirts and pants that had been tossed in without any attempt at folding. There were hand-lettered stickers attached to each bin; by bending down and squinting, she could just make them out. "Dresses, Ladys," one read. "Shirts, Mis-scelanous," said another. Behind the bins were smaller bins with unmatched shoes. Everything had a price tag on it. All the prices had been crossed out in red ink at least once, most had been lowered three or four times.

At first, Elaine was under the impression that the store ended here, then she realized there was another room, down a ramp and to the left. There was no clothing in this room. Its glass-enclosed cabinets were lit by stuttering fluorescent bulbs, guarded by a man reading a newspaper who didn't even look up when she came in.

Elaine was interested, as she always was in anything old. One cabinet was completely given over to wrist watches, another to jewelry, another to cigarette lighters, another to military decorations. She went to each cabinet in turn, brushing away the dust on the glass. When she got to the last one, she saw that there was still another corridor that led to a storeroom of some kind; it seemed to be the only part of Mario's that was adequately lighted. Where before she had had to squint to see in the dark, she now had to shade her eyes, and it was several minutes before she realized the extent of what she was looking at.

The room was lined with high metal shelves that extended all the way to the ceiling, each one crowded with past things. There didn't seem to be any logic in the way they were arranged. Ancient typewriters sat next to old clocks, tattered collections of magazines were stacked by old clothes, hairless teddy bears sat on the laps of armless dolls.

As Elaine walked down aisle after aisle, she began to feel a little sick. What could be done with these discarded, impersonal memories? Whom had they belonged to? They scared her. It was like a nightmare in which all the past things she had worked on with such care had ended up on dusty shelves, a past without people. She took out Olga's fabric and began running back to the ramp that led to the clothing bins. She was out of breath when she reached them, but she fell on her knees before the one marked "Pants, Mens," plunging her arm in it up to the shoulder, groping through layers of rough, scratchy wool until her hand reached the bottom and brushed against the coarsest weave of all.

"Hey, nice pants!" the man at the door said when she paid for them. *"Nice* pants. Who's the lucky guy, lady?"

It was after six by the time Elaine got to Olga's. She rang the bell three times, and Olga peeked suspiciously out the window before letting her in.

"Hello, Olga."

"Well, well, well. Hello yourself, stranger. Come in out of the cold."

"I can't stay long."

"That's what you always say. You forget your old friends for months, then you come in just to say hello good-by. Take your coat off, put your bag on the table."

Elaine had considered a dozen different ways to tell Olga during the bus ride down from the Bronx. Now, in her anxiety, she automatically chose the worst.

"Well, Olga," she said with a little laugh, "you certainly gave me quite an assignment with that piece of cloth. I've had tough jobs before, but not like this."

The moment she saw the embarrassed look on Olga's face, she regretted her words and spoke seriously.

"I know this woman in the Bronx, Olga. She's a genius when it comes to matching fabric. I took it up to her, but she thought I was joking. She didn't know about the camps, Olga. About what happened there. You'd be surprised how many people haven't heard about them. They take these polls among teenagers, and . . . I'm not trying to make excuses for her, but . . . she laughed at me, Olga."

"Go on," Olga said.

"Well, on the way back I passed this old clothing store. I never saw so many old things. They'd just been dumped there over the years in these huge piles. There was a man there. He must have thought I was crazy. I got down on my hands and knees to go

163

through the bins. That's where I found it. Right there in the Bronx."

Elaine took the pants out and held Olga's original small square up against one leg so that Olga could see how well they matched. She didn't know quite what she expected from her. People often became very emotional when she handed them something. Once a man had kissed her hand when she returned his dead wife's wedding gown. Sometimes people cried. But Olga gave no sign of any emotion, happy or sad.

"Very nice," she said. "How much do I owe you?"

"Why . . ."

"I have money. How much?"

"But is it all right?" stammered Elaine. "It does match, doesn't it?"

Olga reached for the pants, looked at them, rubbed them, then handed them back to Elaine.

"I'd like to pretend, Elaine. I can't. I can't take a lie and pretend it's true. Would you respect me if I did that?"

"It's not a lie!"

"No? Look at them."

Elaine shook her head. She knew without looking at them that the pants couldn't fool anyone. Like the major, Olga remembered honestly, without the sentimental cloud that obscured the vision of her other clients. Elaine realized for the first time how much her repairs depended on that cloud. Without it, she was helpless. Without it, the pants were tattered gray wool, nothing more.

"It's no use," Olga said. "And even if you do have something to remember with, the good parts don't last. The bad parts last no matter what. The wrong people remember. The wrong people forget. . . . You wait here."

She left the living room. When she came back, she had her purse.

"Here, you take this money and put it in your pocket for a rainy day. Thank you for trying, Elaine. It was nice knowing you.

Remember me to your mother, please. Tell her Louise says hello."

"She's much better lately," Elaine said mechanically.

"One of these days you'll meet a nice man and get married. You send your old friend a wedding invitation. All right? Maybe a few sniffles, maybe a nice cry? You'll remember?"

Elaine nodded and got up to go; there seemed to be nothing else to do. As they walked toward the door, she noticed an overturned plastic bowl on the floor near the stairs.

"Where's Katya, Olga? She's been hiding ever since I got here."

Olga pushed the dish away with her shoe.

"He remembered, Elaine. The boy who beat her. He remembered all this time. He and his gang. Like a dummy I let her out two nights ago all by herself. Usually I stay on the stoop and watch her, only it was so cold. . . . But these big shots. They had their revenge with her. They left her lying on the stoop in the morning with their swastika trademark painted on the step. It was in the papers. You didn't see it? Toward the back near the sports. Another anti-Semitic outrage, it said. Poor father. I can hear him now. 'But we're not Jews!' "

Olga spoke very calmly. She didn't cry. She didn't act upset. She smiled, and to Elaine the smile was like being slapped in the face.

"It's not your problem, Elaine. She was only a cat. Here, you take the pants and ask for your money back, tell them they were too big for your boyfriend. You keep the fabric, too."

"I can't, Olga. It's yours."

"Keep it or throw it away. All I want to do now is forget. . . . Good-by, Elaine. I wish you happiness always."

The next thing Elaine remembered clearly was sitting alone in a subway car under an advertisement for an abortion clinic, trying to block out her unhappiness and confusion by concentrating on the one image of the past she treasured most: the time her father had taken her to Manhattan thirty years before, the way he had laughed at her excitement as the car swayed back and forth on the tracks.

"If only you could have known him, John," she whispered, hugging her mother's coat to her body in the cold.

She heard herself whisper it, but only with one half of her, the half that had eavesdropped on her dreaming self in the morning. It frightened her, the same way the glimpse of herself in the coffee-shop mirror had frightened her. She remembered the doctor she had seen about her mother who explained how easy it was for the chemicals that controlled the mind to become unbalanced. She remembered the bars on the window of the home she had left her mother in overnight.

"Four more stops to go," she said out loud, trying to concentrate on something simple and real. "Three more stops . . . Two more stops . . ."

Next to the abortion clinic's was another ad, this one from a volunteer crisis center with a phone number you could call for help in emergencies. She wrote it down on a piece of paper, but the moment she got out of the subway she threw it away. She needed someone who knew her, not a disembodied voice. She needed to talk to someone her exact age who had known John.

When she got home she went through the pile of old magazines she kept in the living-room closet until she found the one Rod Martins had written his phone number on that past August. The first time she dialed, the line was busy. When she tried again, a woman answered. Mr. Martins had moved, she said. No, he hadn't left his new number. No, he hadn't left any forwarding address.

Elaine decided it had been foolish of her to call. If anyone was going to comfort her that night, it would have to be John himself. She went into the workshop for one of his unopened letters to Kathy and brought it upstairs to her bedroom where she could read it lying down. She thumbed through it first to see how many pages it was, then quickly skimmed the ending.

"So, good-by college. I'm still not sure what happens next. I'll write you as soon as I know. Say hi to everyone for me. Love, John."

Elaine remembered what Rod Martins had said about John getting kicked out of college. Was this his explanation? With the feeling that he was writing to her and her alone, she began to read the letter.

12

"Remember?" John wrote, "Remember how when we were kids the best thing that could happen was snow? Listening to the weather forecast the night before, watching the thermometer fall, praying it wouldn't change to rain? We didn't have to run away from home to find it. We didn't have to join the Mickey Mouse Club or be Davy Crockett or Superman. The snow came to *us*. And there was no school. We could pull the blankets over our heads and sleep as long as we wanted, which turned out to be a whole extra five minutes we were so excited. At least I was. I used to build igloos in the drifts against the garage. I'd bring Dad's old knapsack in with me and my BB gun and sit there with this long scarf I'd gotten for Christmas wound around my neck waiting to be attacked. Don't laugh, but that's probably why I stayed in college as long as I did. The snow, I mean. Even though I was just going through the motions, there was always enough snow around to remind me of that secret adventure I was getting ready for as a kid. I'd sit there in class, bored as hell, looking out the window at the storm clouds moving in from the mountains, always expecting they'd somehow change everything once they got there. I suppose all of us did after a while. We got so we wanted one big clap of thunder, not snow. But snow's all we ever got. Even before winter carnival started last year, I knew it was time to leave.

"The funny thing is, Byrne and I were innocent bystanders. At least at first. We were way past the winter carnival stage by then. To the rest of the campus it was the greatest thing since rock-'n-roll. Each fraternity made these gigantic snow sculptures illustrating the carnival theme. Last year's was "An Affair to Remember.' Competitive? *Incredibly.* I'd walk past Fraternity Row and see them out there sculpting away in all kinds of weather, one guy directing things with a bull horn like it was the pyramids or something. I was at the stage where I hated all that. The fraternity men, especially. All I could think about was their rich parents, how they had bought their sons expensive cars and expensive schools and got the politicians to protect their investments with 2-S deferments while everyone whose parents didn't have money were getting blown away. I used to get really mad, and then it would hit me . . . Jesus, that's me! I'm no better than they are. If anything my parents are even richer, and I'm hiding behind the same damn deferment that's shielding them. There was only one difference. I knew what a hypocrite I was. The rest of them made snide jokes about the farmers and dropouts who were getting drafted.

"Byrne and I were rooming off-campus by then. Across the street was a rundown Victorian mansion. Used to be the town's only bordello, at least that's what everybody claimed. A lot of independents lived there, which is why it had the reputation of being the center of everything radical at school. Radical, at least for small town Vermont, circa 1966. Even A.P.B. himself wouldn't have much to do with them. He claimed they were queers.

"The week of carnival they decided to build their own snow sculpture just to show up the fraternity men. They built it during the night on the front lawn near the sidewalk. It was an Asian peasant woman with a coolie's hat on her head. She was tilting sideways to protect a little peasant boy and girl who huddled against her. Around the woman's neck was a sign that said 'AN AFFAIR TO REMEMBER.' Over her heart they poured ketchup.

"It was a while before anyone noticed. That weekend was the judging. Everyone was too busy boozing it up to worry about what the long-haired freaks were making downtown. There was a warm spell the beginning of the week. The peasant woman melted a bit.

It made the whole thing more yielding. More abstract. The first mention was an editorial in the college newspaper calling upon future winter carnival committees to issue snowman permits in order to prevent 'misinformed, immature expressions of anarchy.' The local paper in town picked up on it next. They printed a photo of her on the front page. Along with it was a caption asking what was going on with pampered college kids these days. The snow lady was a deliberate insult to the moral sensibilities of the townspeople. Even worse, she was obscene.

"The guys who made her lost interest once the carnival was over. They're the kind who are interested in gestures, not consequences. So Byrne and I adopted her. We'd go down in the morning and patch up whatever damage was inflicted during the night, patting on fresh snow to cover the holes, sweeping up beer bottles the rednecks had thrown at her, etc. Don't ask me why. I think I felt sorry for her more than anything. Like that time you and I were kids and went to see *Bambi*. All these years without knowing it I was going around waiting for a chance to rescue Bambi from the hunters. It was different with Byrne. The angrier the town became, the happier Byrne was. After a while everyone naturally assumed we were the ones who originally built her, which was fine with him. I remember one morning we were pulling glass out of her leg with pliers when this old man, he must have been ninety, came teetering up the sidewalk. He stood there watching us. 'You young fellas build that?' Byrne interrupted me before I could tell him no. 'Yeah. What's the matter with it, grandpa?' The man walked across the snow. He put his face right up close to the peasant lady's to see better. He reached down to pat her children on their heads. For a minute I thought he was going to hand them dimes. 'Well, I'll tell you this, boys. I don't agree with it. No sir. Not here, not in this town. But if that's the way you feel, you go right ahead. It's still a free country no matter what they say.'

"She was there all winter. We rigged up a little awning to keep the sun off her. The ketchup had a way of turning brown. We started using paint instead. It ran down the sides and stained her children, but Byrne said it was better that way. People were getting madder. There was nothing else in the newspaper any more. It was an affront, a deliberate provocation, a mockery of patriotism. There's a lodge hall in town. One night there was a lot of drinking there. When the meeting broke up, they all headed up Main Street toward the river. They picked up some dead branches on the way. There was a lot of shouting. By the time Byrne and I got outside, it was too late to do anything. They had our peasant lady surrounded. Probably twenty of them in the first group. One guy held a spotlight on her, the kind poachers use jacking deer in the mountains. Another guy stood near the door of the house to keep anyone inside from interfering. But what was strange was that about ten minutes went by before they did anything. Here's what I think happened. They expected to find something ugly, like graffiti in a john or an obscene poster. Seeing how beautiful she looked in the white light probably threw them. And she really did look beautiful, too. You should have seen her. It was like she needed real danger all along to bring out her courage and nobility.

"Finally one of the men who was drunker than the rest got up the nerve to throw a whiskey bottle at her head. All hell broke loose. They were on her just like that, swinging their sticks, screaming. One of the guys upstairs must have called the cops. They parked along the curb with their red U-lights flashing, but they didn't do much to break it up. They stamped their feet to keep warm. They called out jokes to friends they recognized in the crowd. Pretty soon practically the entire town was there, pointing and yelling like a crowd at a prize fight.

"It was a shambles in the morning. All the shrubbery trampled. The beer cans piled into three mock headstones near the porch. When Byrne and I went over, it was like poking through the scene of Custer's Last Stand. 'Holy shit!' I remember him yelling. 'A survivor!'

"I wouldn't exactly call her a survivor, but at least you could recognize the patch of snow where the little girl had been. Her mother was ground apart into red bits, her brother's head was kicked off, but somehow we managed to pat her back into shape again. Byrne went through the debris until he found the coolie's hat and hung it around her neck. He started shouting. 'Good peace-loving citizens. Backbone of the nation. Noble pioneers. God-fearing Puritan stock. Still have any illusions about where this town's head is at, Mr. Powers? It must be quite a shock to those Eagle Scout sensibilities of yours.'

"Guess it was. I felt some of Byrne's anger. Enough anyhow to go along with him later on. But more than anything I felt just plain confused. The garbage, the dirty footprints. It was like tea-leaves or the Rosetta stone. The whole future was there for all of us if I could only read the signs right. The snow lady had more significance destroyed than she had whole.

"We didn't waste any time once it got dark. Byrne bought a can of red paint at the hardware store. I borrowed a trowel from our landlady, the kind she used for plants. Our first stop was the police station on Main Street. There's a small yard in the back. We crawled past the window on our bellies until we came to a spot where they'd be sure to see it come morning.

"We had it down to a science by the time the night was over. I'd roll the snow up into three lumps, big, bigger, biggest. One right next to the other. Byrne would smooth them down into roughly the right shape. I'd take off my glove, trace some detail with my finger while Byrne opened the paint. Coolie hats being hard to find in Vermont, we used aluminum foil instead. After six or seven we got so we could bang out a complete sculpture in under five minutes. Not as big as the original naturally. Maybe two and a half, maybe three feet high at the most. I'm not sure how many places we finally hit. The town hall, the lodge hall, the

Congregational Church, the frats, etc. By the time we were done, it was still only midnight. We decided to start building them in people's backyards. We had lots of paint left. Byrne was still mad.

"It started snowing. It was wet snow, easy to pack. Neither of us said very much. We still had to be careful about dogs barking. All the house lights were off. We didn't bother crawling any more. But the more peasants we built, the less enthusiastic I was about building them. It was like I was seeing a hidden side of the town that night. Like I was getting to know the people sleeping inside in a way I hadn't been able to those other three years. From the front the houses all have that buttoned-up look of a Vermont hill town in winter. From the back it's different. There's all kinds of stuff in those backyards. Snowmobile parts, broken sewing machines, sleds, chain saws, big chunks of firewood piled against these old-fashioned porches wrapped in plastic to keep out the cold. I thought about the confusion the people inside would feel when they woke up in the morning and saw the peasants. How they'd have to explain to their kids. I thought about the ashamed look I saw on people's faces that afternoon when they hurried by the yard where the snow lady had been. Remember the old man who told us to go ahead with her? I thought about him.

"Byrne's attitude changed during the night, too. He'd been very methodical at first, very cool. But I think as it got late and the snow started covering up the peasants no matter how high we built them, he began realizing the futility of what we were trying to do. We were just starting another, were on our knees rolling the snow into blocks, when I saw him shake his head, get up, run toward the front of the house. Next there's a lot of cursing. When I got there, he was kicking a kid's snowman to smithereeens. 'For God's sake, Albert! I yelled. 'What in hell do you think you're doing?'

" 'What does it look like, hero?'

"That's all he said. His beard was frozen solid now. The muscles on his face quivered. It was like there was a switch inside him marked *Hate* that something had just flipped on. He wouldn't bother with the peasants anymore. At each house we came to he'd go searching for the kids' snowman, cursing it, kicking it, pissing on the broken pieces once he was done. He was frenzied in the same way the mob had been. He stole a hockey stick from one of the porches to use hacking the snowmen. I tried to take it away from him. That only started him cursing more. We'd made a giant circle during the night, back to our street just as it started getting light out. We were running now. We took a shortcut right through the front yard of the old bordello. Right past the little peasant girl still standing where we had put her.

"Byrne let me run on ahead. When I came back to see what was holding him up he was standing directly over her, straddling her, panting, out of breath. Before I knew what was happening, he swung the hockey stick up like a sword and smashed it down on top of her head. 'Dirty yellow bitch!' He kept hitting her, hitting her. I tried grabbing the stick away again. He swung it at me this time, screaming something I couldn't understand. I went crazy after that. I grabbed him by the collar, picked him up off the ground just as easily as if he were a two-year-old. I started shaking him, slamming my fist into his face as hard as I could. He fell over backward and went rolling over the beer cans. I thought at first I'd killed him. And know what? Know what I've been trying to tell you all along? It was the clap of thunder I'd felt building up inside of me all those years. It was a turning point, the kind that's so unmistakable you realize it really *is* a turning point while it's still happening. All the schools I went to, all the advantages, and where did it lead me? To flattening out my best friend with my fist. It was like I was smashing myself, not Byrne. It was like killing my old self and giving birth to my new self all in the same motion.

"Byrne was on his feet by now. He was holding snow against the cut where I hit him. He was smiling, nodding, like I'd just proved something he'd known all along. 'Welcome to reality, hero,' he said. He started across the street. 'Well, come on! You and I are finished in this town, pal!'

"It didn't take long to pack. I hadn't really bothered *un*packing in the fall. I was so certain something would happen to make me leave. There were some Band-Aids in the bathroom closet. I made Byrne put a couple on. On the way out I left twenty bucks in the landlady's mailbox for the rest of the month's rent. Byrne didn't leave a dime. The bus stop was outside of a diner at the other end of town. We walked there through the snow. It was coming down harder than ever. A waitress sold tickets at the cash register. She told us the first bus north was due in ten minutes. 'That's fine,' said Byrne. He took out his wallet. 'Two to Montreal.'

" 'One,' I said. Byrne looked at me. He turned back to the waitress. 'Two to Montreal.' He said it a lot louder this time. 'My handsome friend here isn't quite right in the head this morning.'

"But that's where he was wrong. I never saw things better in my life. You know what it was like? Like this huge avalanche was skipping down a mountain at me and all I had to do to get out of its way was duck, let it fly over my head and clobber someone else. But what I'm trying to explain is I didn't *want* to duck. I didn't want someone holding a net under me every time the cold cruel world gave a shove. The thing Byrne couldn't understand was that you can drown yourself in the mainstream just as easily as you can in a ditch. There are a lot of ways to shatter your past. Byrne thought there was only one. Before the girl could hand the tickets to him, I took one and put it back on top of the cash register. 'That's not the way I'm going, Albert.'

"He argued with me. He told me not to be a fool. He told me we couldn't stay there. We were draft bait. Cannon fodder. The only place for us was Canada. He said there were hard times coming, and it was as good a place as any to wait them out. He said the whores up there were real nice. Real nice. Real cheap.

"All I said was 'Send me a postcard, Albert.'

"He shrugged. He paid for his ticket. The waitress sold me a ticket to New York. I hadn't figured out where I'd go after that. Head out West until the draft board caught up with me, see the country, etc., this time without the fancy resorts. I was trying to remember how beautiful things had seemed that day on Lake Champlain. I was trying to imagine what I would do if my parents weren't who they were and I wasn't who I was. But I don't think Byrne thought I was serious. I went out with him when the Montreal bus came in. I held my hand out to him but he wouldn't take it. The last I saw of him he was standing on the steps as the door closed. He was looking down at me, shaking his head. 'What a waste. What a goddamn waste.' "

The image of John she had from the letter was so close to the image of John in her dream that she couldn't remember the exact moment she had left off reading and fallen asleep. One moment she felt as though she were with John at the bus stop, the next she was sitting next to him on the bus, asking him questions his letter had raised. Was that really the way things had been? The bitterness, the confused motives and betrayals? She remembered passing a demonstration near the State House in Boston the same year John had protected his snow lady. She had sympathized with the militants' aims but disliked them as people, seeing in their frenzy the same kind of intolerance that caused wars in the first place. But as with all her impressions of those years, it had been brief and incidental. Like John, she had been on her way to the bus station, but only to buy herself a ticket home.

There were no answers in the dream. When she woke up, she saw that someone had covered her with a blanket during the night. The shade had been pulled up. There was a glass of pineapple juice on the table next to the bed.

"What time is it?"

"It's after eight, Elaine. Didn't you hear the alarm?"

Mrs. Collier was standing over the stove with a spatula, poking at something in the frying pan. Seeing her mother cook breakfast seemed part of the dream from which she had just torn herself away. As if in a dream, her mother no longer wore her usual blue suit but had gone into the hall closet for the plaid dress Elaine had bought her for her birthday two years before.

"I get so sick of that same old color," she said, turning around so Elaine could see how well it fit. "You don't think it's too short, do you?"

"It's fine. You look very nice. Can I fix some eggs?"

Mrs. Collier shook her head. "Sit down, Elaine. I'm making French toast this morning. My special way, with cinnamon. Can you eat four slices?"

"I'm not all that hungry, Mommy. We have to be at the clinic at nine."

"That's why I worried when I saw you sleeping. You should try to get to bed earlier. It's not good for you staying up so late. When I went to the bathroom last night, your light was still on."

"It's because I have so much work to finish right now. But I'll be done soon, and then we can take a vacation somewhere. Just you and me. Would you like that? It's been ages since the two of us have gone anywhere."

Mrs. Collier laid the spatula down on a paper towel, came over and rested her hand against Elaine's cheek the way Major Haig-Brown had when he said good-by to her that last afternoon in the hall.

"It's hard on you, isn't it, my love? Taking care of your poor old mother. Working. Not having any friends."

She slid her hand around Elaine's neck until she was stroking her hair.

"It used to be such pretty hair," she said. "I remember I used to comb it in the morning before you went to school, then again at night when you went to bed. A hundred times. Remember that, Elaine? Ninety-eight, ninety-nine, one hundred! Then you would kiss me. Remember? Remember how Johnny would come racing in to say his prayers when we were done? How he would sit there on the bed teasing you about how long your hair was? Remember that, Elaine?"

Elaine turned abruptly away.

"It's time to go," she said.

"We must keep up our strength for him. He'll be done college soon. We must keep everything just the way he remembers so he won't be disappointed when he gets home. I'll comb your hair for you. Would you like that, Elaine? I'll comb it just like I used to when you were small."

When they got to the clinic, her mother went into the doctor's office alone, without the little tug-of-war in the corridor that had been an embarrassing part of their usual routine. Elaine sat in the lobby with the other daughters, comparing her lack of hope with theirs, wondering if her face seemed as tired and hard. There was a woman named Ruby she had gotten to know. Each week she gave Elaine another installment of her life history; this week's was about the time her first husband had left her. Elaine listened patiently as she always did, wondering if Ruby would be interested in hearing about Mr. Powers. Even as recently as a month ago, Elaine would have given anything to have someone to talk to about him, even a stranger, but now she wasn't so sure. How could she begin to explain how things stood between them when she didn't know herself? Even if she could explain, was it worth it any more? She had thought about him less and less since Christmas, and when she did, it was only in connection with John.

Her mother came out before Ruby's story was done. Elaine excused herself. She took her mother to the clinic's coffee shop for lunch.

"I think I'll have the chicken salad," Mrs. Collier told the waitress. "Chicken is my son's favorite food."

She spent the entire lunch telling Elaine how lucky she was to have a brother like John. She told the waitress, too, when she came over to clear their table. She kept it up all the way home. The bus driver, the man at the newspaper stand, Mrs. Peabody sprinkling her tiny garden next door, each of them heard about how lucky she was to have John.

The phone in the office was ringing when they got home. Elaine waited until her mother was safely started up the stairs, then rushed in to answer it, but by the time she got there whoever it was had hung up. She sat there for a few minutes in case it rang again. When she came back into the hall she was surprised to find that her mother was still there. She was standing by the front door with a letter in one hand. She was frowning.

"The mailman came while you were gone," she explained. "It was a different mailman this time. He gave me this."

It was a package from Mr. Powers with some of John's last letters. Mrs. Collier had already opened one. She shook her head back and forth as if something dreadful had happened.

"Oh, dear," she said at last. "The strangest thing, Elaine. Your brother John has gone to be a soldier."

"What?" Elaine asked.

"The army, Elaine. John's serving his country now, just like his father did."

She said it with the same proud conviction in her voice that had been there on the night that she had first referred to him as her son. Elaine had made the mistake then of thinking that she could talk her out of it. Now, she knew better. Her mother needed an explanation. Elaine decided to tell her the truth.

"John left college, Mommy. He wasn't happy there. He decided to let himself be drafted."

Her mother looked puzzled. Elaine tried again. "He decided to fight for his country."

Her mother smiled. She started nodding. "Like his father."

"Yes, Mommy. Now do you think you could let me have the rest of those? It's time for your nap. I'll show them to you as soon as you wake up."

"Do you promise, Elaine? I am feeling a bit tired right now. You read them and tell me what they say. I hope he's all right. It is strange, isn't it? You'd think he would have mentioned something before this."

Her mother handed her the package and started up the stairs. "Mother?"

Mrs. Collier stopped and turned around. "Yes, Elaine?"

"John is in the army now," she said gently. "You know what that means, don't you? He may have to go overseas."

"Overseas?"

"They may need him somewhere where there's fighting. They may send him there some day."

"Where?" asked Mrs. Collier.

Elaine hesitated, trying to make out her mother's face on the dark stairs.

"To Vietnam," she said at last.

"Where?"

"Vietnam."

"That's not Korea, is it?" her mother said, suddenly frightened. She started to sob. "They wouldn't send him to Korea, would they?"

It was too much for Elaine—her mother's alarm, her own fear of saying something she shouldn't. She ran up the stairs and took hold of her mother's hand.

"No, Mommy," she said reassuringly. "Korea is all over with now. We'll talk about it some other time, okay? Will you be all right if I stay down here?"

Her mother had control of herself now. She put her hand against Elaine's cheek the same way she had at breakfast.

"He's not in any danger yet," she said soothingly, as if it were her turn to do the comforting. "He's just joined up, Elaine. It will be a long time yet before they can send him anywhere."

"That's right, Mommy," Elaine said. "Let's not worry about it. I feel a lot better now."

Elaine waited until her mother was all the way upstairs before she went into her office to examine the letter. It was a short one, written to his parents from an army camp in Georgia. "I'm okay," it said. "I feel much better about things now. Trust me, John." The next letter in the package was an unopened one to Kathy. He had completed basic training. His test scores were so high the

Army had sent him to OCS in Maryland, then to another camp in California.

"I fit in here," he wrote. "It's like being on a team again but without all that rah-rah, eat-em-up bullshit they gave us in school. There's lots of gung-ho stuff around but not in this regiment, thank God. That's the one thing I couldn't handle. Know something? I think maybe deep down inside I'm jock enough to have missed all this. The pulling together I mean. The kidding around, pushing yourself past your limit, etc. If you could see the look on my guys' faces on maneuvers when they're tired or ready to give up, reaching back to give just a little more of themselves, pulling together for something no matter how stupid it is. Take my word for it, they're the only ones left in this damn country who know what the word *together* means any more. Jones is the only one giving me trouble. Cpt. Reynolds told me he was a trouble-maker when I first got him. If he wasn't in, he'd be slashing people in Watts, at least that's what Reynolds says. He goes around telling everybody they were fools for getting drafted. He was getting pretty bitter there for a while, but I think I'm starting to get through to him.

"Chicken again last night. The *same* chicken. I recognized the wings.

"Rumor has it we'll be making a move on out of here pretty soon. Into the Valley of the Jaws of Death. Yea for I will fear no evil, volleyed and thundered, the outlook wasn't brilliant for the Mudville nine that day. My God! That's practically all the poetry I know. What is it about the army that makes you start reading poetry you never gave a damn about in school?

"If nothing else, the guys respect me. It's a great feeling, the one I've been after right along. If you told them my father was worth a couple of million they wouldn't believe it. They'd laugh in your face. Sometimes they come to me to talk over some of their problems. We sit around bullshitting and they ask where I'm from and so on. I tell them how my old man's just retired from owning this drugstore back in Bridgeport, how he was wounded on Okinawa, etc. I really build it up. Tell them about my mom and sister, go into this big thing about how we used to go on picnics out in the country in my old man's Ford. Dad has a limp on account of the shrapnel. Mom's a little nearsighted with nice gray hair. Sis is always teasing me about my girlfriends. We get along fine, all four of us . . ."

Elaine put the letter down. "My mom and sister." She read it again. "My mom and sister . . ." She remembered the first time he had mentioned a make-believe family in talking to his friend Byrne, but she had taken it then the way he had obviously intended it, as a joke. But here it was again in a letter written several years later.

She thought about it the rest of the day. Had John in some mysterious way needed them even more than they needed him? It was like the missing part in a jigsaw puzzle—it explained why he blended so well with her pictures, why his letters seemed increasingly those a brother might send his sister. Even his being in the army in the first place seemed more natural that way. There was no possibility whatever of the John in the films and scrapbooks the Powers had originally sent her being drafted. In the new John of her own past, it seemed the most natural thing in the world. John the dropout at loose ends, posed against a background of cheap amusement parks and dirty beaches. John the misfit growing up surrounded by two women who doted on him. John anxious to assert his virility and independence once and for all. Seen like that, what became surprising was that he had escaped for so long. How had that John managed to get to college in the first place? How had that John avoided the draft for even the short time that he had?

Later in the week another package arrived, this one with more letters and a few random souvenirs. Elaine noticed at once that John's handwriting had changed, the words had become smaller, more tightly bunched. His spelling was careless, and there was less introspection, fewer attempts to explain. Even the envelopes the letters came in were different now. They were airmail envelopes, the thin kind, looking wrinkled and soiled. The souvenirs he sent home looked the same: second-hand, infected, potential carriers of contagious disease. There were the American-flag pins he bought in San Diego, with the stripes flaking off; maps to hang on the wall to follow where he was, with the borders of countries obliterated by green ink, the continents separated by constant refoldings. There were stuffed animals he had bought at the base P.X. for Mother's Day, shedding fur; brightly colored scarves he found in Saigon during leave, with a cloying, nutlike smell.

Mrs. Collier wore her scarf everywhere, fastened around her neck with the American-flag pin. The toy kitten and toy lamb sat on her bedroom dresser facing the mirror; the map was pasted across the refrigerator door. By the time Elaine woke up in the morning, her mother would have already hurried downstairs to take Mr. Powers's latest package from the mailman's hands.

"I wish you'd let me open them first," Elaine said peevishly. "You know I always show them to you."

But her mother was too excited to listen. "Here's one, Elaine! I knew it when I woke up this morning. I knew there would be at least one letter for us before Easter. Do you think you could read it out loud to me, my love? I've left my glasses upstairs."

Elaine took it from her and, in a hurry to be done with it, started reading the page halfway down:

" 'But I just wanted to let you know everything is fine with me. This is a country club compared to what most platoons are getting stuck with right now. It's perfectly safe where we are, so please don't worry about me. The guys play football all day. Sometimes Goldman and I take the jeep into town. You see a lot of things over here you just wouldn't believe. Elections last week. *Elections*, right? Patrols sweeping through these bars, dragging junkies off to vote, slapping them around with their gun butts until they're sober enough to put their X's where they're told. Hope the ones we meet up on the line are a lot more Morale-Inspiring, if you know what I mean. Anyway, that's about all for now. Tomorrow we're moving up so it might be a while until you hear from me. Don't worry because I'll write as soon as I can. Maybe I'll call you Easter. Be home? The U.S.O. has these special lines set up. I'll probably be so nervous I won't know what to say, but maybe you won't mind five minutes' worth of stammering. And don't forget, when I get home I'm going to take you out to the best Italian restaurant in New York. Fettucine, saltimboca, lots of good wine. Deal? Love, John.' "

"Is that all, Elaine? He usually puts a P.S. on the end."

"Love, John. There's no P.S. on this one, Mommy. Are you happy now? Will you be all right by yourself for a while? I have to get some work done, then I'll come upstairs and fix your lunch."

"He always did like Italian food. He always called it pisghetti, even when he knew better. He would never pronounce cinammon right either, just to tease me. Are you sure there isn't more?"

His letters became bitter after Easter. He complained about the government tying their hands, complained about the peasants who would set themselves on his men in ambush, the children pushed out first to draw their fire; about the land mines they would trip over when they went in after snipers, how one of his men bled to death in a clearing without anyone being able to help. He used more slang in these, became crudely bigoted, reminding her of the macho, profane boys she had grown up with—the goddamn mud, the goddamn heat. He was tired of it, he said. He'd been crazy letting them draft him. Two years of his life down the drain. All he could think about was home. His hitch would be up soon, and he would go back to school for his degree.

"Do you think he will, Elaine?" her mother asked when Elaine was trying to get her to bed. "Come home soon now? Home for good this time?"

"Shh, Mommy. Time to go to sleep."

"Remember when the three of us went to the beach? The picnic we had there on the sand near the boardwalk?"

"Here, let me fix the blankets for you."

"The time I took the two of you to Coney Island to ride the merry-go-round? The way Johnny almost fell off?"

"Tomorrow we have to go to the drugstore and have your pills refilled."

"Those were the days, Elaine. I had the two of you to take care of. You were such a help to me, too, times he got sick. You used to stay home from school just so he wouldn't get lonely, sitting there on the rug next to him playing checkers. You were always so much more grown-up than he was. Johnny always had those high spirits of his to get him in trouble. Not real trouble, though. Johnny was a good boy. He was just having his fun is all. He'd never hurt anybody. Not deliberately. . . . Oh, Elaine! Remember how we used to ride the subway in to Central Park to feed the squirrels?"

Elaine nodded. "On Sundays. I remember you used to buy popcorn for them at the station before we left."

"The buttered kind! And it smelled so good we always ended up eating most of it before we got there . . ."

"And then you would give me a quarter to go and buy some more from the man who was always standing by the seal pond with his hot-dog wagon . . ."

"Mr. Scoloni! I remember it was Mr. Scoloni because he always took out pictures of his daughter back in Italy to show me. He was so proud of her. He kept a lock of her hair in an envelope to show people when they bought their hot dogs. You would pay him and bring the popcorn over, and we would start feeding them. All those lovely brown ones who used to come right up and jump across our shoes, only you used to like throwing pieces to the shy ones instead, the ones who held back by the swings and couldn't get up the nerve to come any closer. Remember, Elaine? Remember the way Johnny would run off and play baseball all by himself?

How handsome he looked standing there swinging his bat at acorns you threw him? How mad he would get if he missed?"

"It's getting late, Mommy. Time to go to sleep now."

"Oh, Elaine. We had such good times, didn't we?"

Her voice trailed off into a whisper—a long protesting sigh that ended the moment she closed her eyes. Elaine tucked the blankets under her chin and sat there on the edge of the bed until her mother's breathing became regular and deep.

"I remember," she whispered, leaning over to kiss her on the cheek. "I remember all those things, Mommy. Sweet dreams, my love."

She checked to see the front door was locked before she went through the office to her workshop. It was past midnight, but she wasn't tired. There was one final letter from John to go over before morning. Short as it was, it was the longest he had written in several months, and she needed to be by herself when she first read it. She opened the envelope with the same tarnished butter knife she always used.

"Not much new. Right now I'm sitting in a hole in the ground with a flashlight in one hand, a pen in the other, trying to put together a few lines for you before catching some sleep. We're dug in on a hill, don't ask me where. Somewhere in Asia I suppose. That's where we were last time anyone bothered asking. Tomorrow A.M. we're moving into a village about three miles from here whose name I can't even pronounce, let alone spell. All I know is, it's going to be muddy, it's going to smell. Intelligence claims it's lousy with VC. Lucky us. Only consolation, it can't be any worse than last time. Or so we tell ourselves.

"Nice starry night out. If I stretch out on my genuine U.S. Army waterproof poncho (all the better for wrapping our dead and wounded in, my dear), look directly up at the sky, that's all I see, no trees, no camouflage, just stars. Reminds me of times we used to lie on our backs on the beach looking up at all the different constellations trying to name them. You were always lots better at it than I was. I was pretty good on the Big Dipper, but you had me beat on all the rest. Betelgeuse. God, where in hell did you come up with that one? Wish to hell I could find Betelgeuse now. Sometimes these replacements they send us get jumpy and start firing at shooting stars thinking they're tracers. Haven't hit one yet. Just thought of another one. Sirius. That poem of Frost's you used to read me. 'I'm a poor underdog,/But tonight I will bark/ With that great Overdog that romps through the dark.' Right on!

"I think about you a lot lately. Remembering all the good times we had. Teaching you to swim at the pool. Presents we used to give each other at Christmas. Jesus, I could make a list. Remember that bookstore we used to go to? Mitchell's I think it was called. They used to have a soundproof booth where you could listen to records before you bought them. We thought that was so old-fashioned and cool. I remember you saying we should find a soda fountain afterward and share a chocolate frappé with two straws. But I guess we must have worn out a hundred records between us that weekend. I remember because that Sunday was the last time I saw you. I remember how you looked. Kind of sad, kind of lonely, standing there all by yourself on the sidewalk as if you didn't have a friend in the world. I know, because that's the way I'm feeling right now. Sad and lonely, missing you. All those things we shared. All those adventures we were going to find together. All that love.

"Time to go now. Sorry about that. We defenders of liberty and justice for all, even gooks, can't afford to get misty-eyed. Spoils the aim. If I get a chance, I'll write tomorrow night. Schultz is screaming in his sleep again. Half the men over here are screaming in their sleep tonight, only they're not screaming out loud. You have no idea how bad things are. That bastard Jones bought it yesterday. Caught a short in the groin. Took off both legs. He kept begging us to shoot him. Nobody would while any officers were around. I took a hike up around the fire control center. When I came back, he was dead. Chopper flew him out this A.M. So now what? Am I supposed to write a letter to his folks or what? Dear Mr. and Mrs. Jones, Your son is dead; he was an ass, regretfully, Lieutenant John A. Powers? Nobody tells you a goddamn thing in this division. Body count is all they're interested in. Real super Intelligence, too. They can't even tell us which ones are our gooks, which ones are their gooks. They all look the same. We go into a village, a kid comes up to us in shorts with a bowl of rice, waving a little white flag. Next thing you know we're eating the rice, he's behind a tree lobbing grenades at us. What are we supposed to do, feed him bubble gum? To hell with that. They've got a saying over here that's really true. Scruples kill more guys than land mines. I told the guys that tonight when I explained what the setup was going to be tomorrow when we go in. From now on this platoon's got itself a new rule, I said. When we go into a village if it's yellow and got balls, we shoot first and ask questions later. Fuck division, I said. Fuck Intelligence. Fuck everyone."

There was no signature on the bottom. No P.S. She tore through the clutter on her desk to find the envelope, but there were no extra pages she had missed. She read the letter through six times, forcing herself to imagine what that night on the hill must have been like, sharing it with him.

All her sense of time was gone. If someone had told her it was still midnight, she wouldn't have been surprised. If someone else had told her it was two weeks since she had kissed her mother goodnight, she would have accepted that, too. Before she could read the letter a seventh time, the sun came through the drapes.

"Love, John."

She said it to herself, then said it out loud. It was the only protest she made.

She opened the drapes, squinting, turning away from the brightness. When she got back to the couch, the letter had fallen upside down on the floor. Whatever magic it had had during the night was gone now. She stood there staring at it, wondering where to put it.

There was no room for it in her desk. The drawers already overflowed with his earlier letters; the top was covered with broken models, tarnished trophies she had never had the time to repair. There was no room on the shelves; they were taken up with the scrapbooks and films. It was as though his entire past had deliberately crowded together to refuse this last small addition, censoring it, closing ranks to prevent contamination. She finally decided to make a separate place for it in the cabinet near the work table she saved for those past things that meant most to her. Opening the door to slide it in, her hand brushed against something hard and cold on the bottom shelf: Major Haig-Brown's Somme seed in the same clay pot she had buried it in the week after he died.

She didn't want to deal with it now, she had enough on her mind. She started moving it aside to make room for the letter when she noticed something red jutting up above the edge of the pot. At first she thought her eyes were playing tricks on her. She closed them, looked at it again. There was no mistaking it now. There was something red above the dirt where she had planted the major's seed.

She took it over to the window and set it down on the sill, her hands suddenly cold and trembling. But when she looked at it in the full light, she saw it wasn't a blossom after all. A piece of red Christmas tinsel had fallen off a package on the top shelf where she stored her father's war letters. When she picked up the seed—gently, with no more pressure than was necessary to separate it from the dirt—it disintegrated into dust in her hands. Ludicrously, the dust made her sneeze.

She refused to cry over it. She went back to the cabinet to see if there was any part of the flower she might have missed. But there was nothing. As pure as the major's memory had been, it had left out killing the German soldier for the flower, ensuring that no nostalgic yearning, no tender love, could ever bring the seed back to life. The past had to be remembered totally or not at all—that was the first law. It wasn't the killing of the soldier in 1916 that had poisoned the flower, but the deliberate forgetting of the killing in the long years since.

Next to the space on the shelf where the flower had been was Olga's fabric, the threads starting to unravel. The thinner ones blew onto the floor when Elaine reached in. She had tried to save it just as she had tried to save the flower, but only at the price of taking its burden upon herself. The past needed someone's memory to bring it to life—that was the second law. When Olga turned her back on the fabric, Elaine had been there to inherit it, ensuring a continuum, as if the past were a grand relay race in which a faltering runner passed a baton to a fresher team mate for the next lap around the endless, circular track. No matter who temporarily held it, the past was a constant—changing aspect, at times evaporating into all but undetectable states, but never diminishing, governed by a law of conservation as strict as that governing energy and matter. The past could be transferred or inherited but never obliterated or destroyed—that was the most important law of all. Olga's fabric would continue to fade and unravel until finally it turned into the same dust as the flower. But Elaine would be haunted by it until she died, too, and the past descended to someone else in keeping with all the laws—totally remembered, brought to life, neither obliterated nor destroyed.

In the same meticulous way that she had fussed over the fallen letter, she got the whisk broom to sweep up the dust and lint from the rug. I must do everything very precisely now, she thought. I must not give myself time to worry about John.

She couldn't find the dustpan. There had always been one on the counter near the projector, but for some reason it was gone. There was nothing left but a last pile of newspapers from the late 1960's. She took out a copy from the bottom and bent to sweep the dust onto the outspread front page. In doing so, she noticed that it wasn't as yellow as the older papers she had already worked on. Her eye was caught by a picture below the largest headline.

It was of a little girl. She couldn't have been much over eight or nine. She was naked, screaming, running along a dirt road toward the camera lens, arms flung out to either side as though pinioned on an invisible cross that her pathetically thin ribs just managed to hide. Behind her was a forest, with a tall column of smoke rolling toward the picture's right-hand side. Between her and the trees were more people, in hazier focus—a woman, some smaller children, the smallest of whom was in the process of falling to the ground. But it was the girl on whom the picture centered. Elaine read the caption, registered the words "napalm," "mistake" and "village," but none of these seemed to have anything to do with the terror so evident on the girl's face. As she looked at it, she realized it wasn't a picture of a terrified girl at all. It was a picture of pain itself.

All the pictures were like that now. Pictures of mobs burning flags before buildings with tall, Corinthian columns. Pictures of a black man, then a white man, their blood-soaked heads cradled protectively in supportive arms while frantic men on the edges of the picture pointed off in the directions from which the shots had come. Pictures of a tank in a trampled clearing, flowers stuck in its barrel, the tank crew making the peace sign, laughing, but their weapon looking just as ugly and squat and menacing as ever. Pictures of burning forests, burning cities, blackened fields where no crops were left, blasted streets with no buildings. A grinning army officer pointed his pistol into a prisoner's left ear. A policeman swung his night stick across a girl's breasts as she fought desperately to hold a smudged sign high enough so that the photographer could see it.

Headlines were bigger, inflated type competing for deflated emotions. Even ads were surrounded by black margins; one consisted of an entire page of miniature black crosses, fifty to a line, with lists of names and ages and dates. "Robert Sommers, Age eighteen, Died July 4, 1968 . . . Meritwether Lee, Age nineteen, Died November 17, 1968 . . . Peter Borelli, Age twenty-one, Died Christmas Day, 1968 . . ."

She didn't read all the names. She didn't look at all the pictures. The deadening, numbing process that constant atrocities bred in other people's hearts had been spread across the three or four years the newspapers covered, so that they never realized how hard and indifferent they had become until it was too late. In her heart, the numbing occurred instantaneously, in the few minutes it took to skim through one paper and go on to the next.

She fought the horror, the anger, the numbness. She suddenly thought of the picture of the black woman she had once removed as an experiment—how tranquil the page had seemed afterward. Wasn't it as simple as that? There were dozens of old newspapers she could go back to, an untapped preserve of gentleness and sanity she could draw on to patch up the horror of the papers she was going through now. There were forgotten baseball games played on innocent, grassy fields fifteen years ago; far-off portraits of unassuming farmers standing by record crops of corn and wheat; pictures taken at high-school proms, the girls in bobby sox, the boys in loafers; pictures of children playing catch in unspoiled parks. It would be hard, she would have to hurry, but it could be done. The important thing was time. She would start at the top of the pile and work her way down, tearing out the horror, page by page. That was the important thing. To remove it. She wouldn't replace it with anything else for the moment. The important thing was to hurry. The important thing was time . . .

But she was tired—she couldn't remember how long it had been since she had gotten any sleep. For all her determination she didn't get beyond the first page of the first paper she picked up off the top of the pile. There near the middle was a picture of a soldier lying face down in mud. His arms were flung out to either side in the same way the peasant boy's had been, as though whoever it was had sought this mud all along, throwing himself down to embrace it with the one passionate throb of life that was left to him. Next to the body knelt a medic, but it was obvious that it was no use. Behind him, two soldiers who had picked up a stretcher were putting it back down again. The caption didn't mention any names.

She was still staring at the picture when Mrs. Powers called. She brought it over to the phone with her and never took her eyes off it while Mrs. Powers was speaking.

She was sorry to bother her, Mrs. Powers said. She just wanted to thank her one last time for all her help. The scrapbooks were silly old things really. It was rather sad their going through the films by themselves, they were so empty with only the two of them down through the years. Oh, well . . . They had decided when they were first married not to have children, and they had stuck by that decision. There were so many horrible things in the world they might be exposed to. It was lonely at Christmas, of course, but at least they had been spared the pain so many parents must go through. And Elaine . . . Elaine must certainly spend the weekend with them sometime soon, and her young man, too, if she had one.

Elaine sat there without moving after she hung up. Everything had become part of the same inevitability—the picture, Mrs. Powers's call, her own dull, emotionless acceptance. She couldn't remember the phone actually ringing again. She only remembered picking it up, listening to Mr. Powers's familiar voice, nodding dumbly at what he had to say, putting the phone back down when he was through.

He wanted to tell her how much they owed her, he said. The sixties had been a nightmare for them. He was glad that was all buried in the past now. His wife had changed remarkably. She was young and vivacious again; it wasn't too much to say that Elaine, in phasing their son out of their lives, had given him back the girl he had married. He was very grateful; he'd be sending a check very soon. He'd already sent the last of John's things. . . . She was a fine young woman and would make some man a fine wife. If they had ever had a daughter, it would have been nice to have had one like her . . . He'd bring them down himself but he thought she might interpret it the wrong way. A clean break healed fastest . . . It was wonderful what she'd done for them.

Elaine heard the mailman at the door. She heard him ring a second time, but she still couldn't find the strength to get up. The razor was on the desk beside her. She ran it up and down the margins of the soldier's picture, finally letting it drop on the floor, putting her head down on the desk, hugging herself in the cold.

"Elaine?"

"Go away."

"Elaine, my love?"

Her mother was standing there in the doorway dressed in her robe.

"Elaine! Johnny's come home!"

She carried a brown package in her arms. Gently, as if it were a baby, she placed it on the work table and turned the light on so Elaine could see. There wasn't much inside. A webbed gun belt, a comb and a brush, a wallet, some formal-looking letters on army stationery, pay receipts, a few pieces of loose change.

"Your brother's come home, Elaine! Johnny's come home!"

"Go away, Mommy. Just go away and leave me alone."

"Look and see what he's brought us from Asia, my love!"

"Go away!"

"Look what our Johnny went and brought us!"

And finally she did look, grabbing the package from off the table and tearing through the paper until she found the manila envelope from the Defense Department. She held it up to her mother's face. She forced her to take it in her hand.

"He's dead!" she screamed. "John's dead! Read it!"

"John . . ."

"Read it!"

Her mother did read it—her mother ran crying upstairs to her bedroom just as she had thirty years before. Elaine waited until she heard the door slam, then, very carefully, with the professional thoroughness for which she was known, she took the wallet from the cellophane in which it had been sealed, removed the picture of what she could see now were two old, rather foolish people standing in front of an old, rather grotesquely large home, and replaced it with a much simpler one of her and her mother standing arm in arm by the clinic door.

When she had finished, the pain was theirs, the pain that was always meant to be theirs, and she went upstairs to comfort her mother as best she could.

ABOUT THE AUTHOR

W. D. WETHERELL was born on Long Island and attended school there. His short stories have been published in the *Atlantic, Virginia Quarterly Review,* and the O'Henry Awards collection, as well as other magazines. His articles on travel and the outdoors have appeared in a variety of publications, including *The New York Times. Souvenirs* is his first novel.